Undisclosed

Desire

The Tycoon's Heart

by Falon Gold

Published Assistance by Nayberry Publications (2017)
Opelika, Alabama, 36801, USA

PUBLISHER'S NOTE
This is a work of fiction. Names, characters, places, and incidents either are the product of the author's imagination or are used fictitiously, and any resemblance to actual persons, living or dead, business establishments, events, or locales is entirely coincidental. The publisher does not have any control over and does not assume any responsibility for author or third-party Web sites or their content.

Chapter One

Friday is finally here. In three hours, I board my plane leaving Utah, fly to Vegas, and check into my hotel where I can sleep for the whole weekend if I want to. My boss, Apollo Ford, grudgingly promised me this weekend off, with no emergency calls or unexpected problems. Being the personal assistant to a workaholic investment banker is becoming hazardous to my health. It's too bad Mr. Ford's look—too damn tall, dark, and handsome—doesn't make it easy to work for him either.

His slaver-driver mode can last for days until I can't remember the last time I talked to my family back in Colorado. And I damn sure haven't been able to visit them since I started at Ford Global Enterprises four years ago. This hard work day in and day out is how I lost seventy-five pounds without one visit to a gym. Okay, that aspect isn't so bad. However, the constant dark circles under my eyes, lack of sleep, and a developing case of narcolepsy definitely isn't a positive result from working around the clock. I had to threaten to quit for real before he agreed to give me the next two days off.

Don't get me wrong. He isn't happy about having to fend for himself for forty-eight measly hours at the business that *he* chose to start ten years ago. Therefore, I know I'll have to quit for real, one day. My health and future love life keep begging me to pin a date down.

I'm moving around the office at a fast clip so my weekend away from work and Mr. Ford can start as soon as possible. Readying things for his weekend meetings, like putting reports that he'll need on the right corner of his black lacquer desk with the glass top and stacking takeout menus on the left corner are next to the last things I have to do today. If I find his cell phone, erasing my number out of it is imperative before I fly one state over, or he'll call me morning, noon, and night.

Sigh.

All he needs is one excuse to call and he will. Mostly, he calls because he can't find contracts or payroll timesheets, which I leave in the bin that *he* designated for paperwork that needs his signature. Occasionally, he can't find the list of passwords that are in a locked bottom drawer of his desk every day, all day, even though he has one of the only two keys to it in his pocket at all times. Sometimes, I swear he just likes to hear my sleepy voice, and he's obviously an insomniac. Well, I'm not. I love to get my rest, and I don't appreciate being forced to work around the clock. His workaholic tendencies are running me down physically and making me run from the person I developed a crush on the minute I stepped in his office to interview as his personal assistant. Almost completely blinding love for him crept upon me slowly afterwards. It's part of the reason why I need this break.

When I walk into his office, he's standing at the glass wall, glaring at the view of Lake City. His office is enormous and sparsely decorated with just his and my matching desks. Black file cabinets sit behind each desk, which face each other from opposite ends of the room. His side has the glass wall and a fantastic view of Lake City's skyline.

I can tell he's grumpy about my leaving, but that's just tough. I'm out of here as soon as I open every file on his computer, so he can't call asking about damn passwords.

"Malisa," someone whispers in my ear, startling the hell out of me while I'm bending over the bottom drawer of Ford's desk.

I spring upright, as if I've been caught doing something I shouldn't have. My heart beats erratically.

"*Jesus, Mr. Ford,*" I hiss, wondering when he crossed the room. "Give a girl some warning next time, why don't you?" I say and

I tug my ruffled white blouse down over my plain gray skirt, both two sizes too big and held up by a wide, gray belt.

He takes a seat on the corner of his desk, eyeballing me with dark, bedroom eyes that could convince sugar to jump out of a cake. "You're in a big hurry to leave me, aren't you?" he asks, and I hear pure need in his voice. Not simply the need of his personal assistant, but a need for me.

I drop down into his heavily-cushioned office chair then reach down for the drawer with the passwords again, with him looking down on me. Tingles fire off along the back of my bare neck. If he can affect my skin by just looking at me, what would happen if he ever actually touched it?

I'll never know. I'm not the type of woman he dates, and I'm unwilling to get caught up in his basket of significant others. I quickly push back the fantasy that I'm having about him needing me and jokingly say, "Yes, Mr. Ford, I'm fleeing here like I stole something. I would appreciate if you didn't call me for anything after I'm gone. I left my cell phone at home in case you do, and the hotel won't be allowed to put calls through to my room. I'm taking the phone off the hook just in case they try."

That's partially a lie. I have a wakeup call scheduled for eight a.m. and want my family to be able to reach me if anything happens in Colorado. But after four long years without a real break, I want to be free of Ford Global Enterprises for every moment possible.

Bingo! I retrieve the lists of passwords and sit up to face the computer. He crosses his thick, muscular arms that he keeps toned in the gym three floors above us, with too damn early in the morning workouts.

"I don't know why you have to go all the way to Vegas, Malisa. I know how to leave a woman alone that doesn't want to be bothered with me."

I roll my eyes heavenward then start to open files on the computer. "What woman do you know that doesn't want your company?"

"You," he fires back.

That's not exactly true, but what good would it do me to tell him that?

"Well, that's your fault, Mr. Ford, for working me like a dog. I'll be dead by the time I'm thirty at this rate."

He cocks an eyebrow. "Overdramatic much, Malisa?"

"That's because I don't sleep much, *Ford*," I counter. "You really need to hire another assistant. I know you can afford it, because I print off reports of your bottom line every day."

He shrugs. "What can I say? I'm a busy man."

"One that needs more help."

Mr. Ford starts to do one of his ordinary things that always does weird things to my heartbeat and the bottom of my stomach; he simply grins. "I'm going to miss that mouth of yours," he admits.

"I will not miss yours," I grumble underneath my breath.

At least, I'm going to try not to miss it.

He starts to chuckle quietly, as expected.

Apollo and I are probably the only white male boss and black female employee in the entire state of Utah that get along like a house on fire. He says whatever he wants to me and I return the favor. Nothing sexual has ever passed from his lips toward me, not even when I've slept over his house, which is at least twice a week. I'm there even more nights when there's a difficult client who lives overseas and keeps changing the terms of whatever contract. Eventually, I pass out on Ford's home office's leather couch, and he keeps right on working until he drops at his desk. When he wakes up with keyboard-face and a blanket I've thrown over his shoulders, I'm gone, having slipped out the side door at the crack of dawn. Usually, I make it to my home on the less expensive side of town in my reliable

Honda Civic and have just unlocked my front door before he's barking an order into my phone for me to come back.

Sometimes, I outright refuse. When he threatens to fire me, I tell him to go ahead. Then, he gives me a few hours to sleep, shower, and show up for work. His dry wit keeps me entertained while he orders me around. I don't mind it, especially when what he pays me a month is more than what most personal assistants make in half a year anywhere.

The best part about working for him is that I get paid extremely well for staring into his oval-shaped, chocolate eyes, pondering whether his slightly larger top lip that overlaps his bottom one is as supple as it looks, and imagining running my fingers over his perfectly built body. He's just right, not too big or too slim.

Whether I'm on the clock or at home in my bed alone, my mind always wanders to running my fingers through his hair that I schedule cuts for every two weeks. It's a little long on the top, parted on the right, and swoops backwards, to blend in with the closely-shaved hair around his ears and nape so it doesn't touch the designer suits that he wears.

When I'm asked to make reservations for the classiest of restaurants, so he can enjoy himself with other women, I get a little grumpy and a lot heartbroken, but he's never noticed. If I had time to schedule my own dates, maybe I wouldn't be so crabby about him wining and dining some socialite from one continent or another.

They're always beautiful women that know the difference between Prada and Gucci, and that's about all. Ford seems to like his women shallow, so I don't hold out any real hope for spending time with him that doesn't involve his computer, business, or dry-cleaning. I'm officially work-zoned in his world, and my battery-operated boyfriend isn't enough to remove Apollo from my deepest needs and thoughts anymore. So, I will *have* to find another job or a date soon.

I need more than my fantasies of him can provide, and I want it all: the house with the picket fence, two point five kids, and even the damn dog. I've been picky about the men I dated since I left college, which means I haven't been dating. Okay, maybe I've been secretly waiting for Apollo to ask me out.

It's time to stop waiting and start dating again, beginning with a spa visit and complete makeover at the Shalimar Hotel in Vegas.

With the fat that was hugging my short frame like icing on a cake gone, I can now flaunt whatever figure I got, after I get rid of the oversized clothes I've been housing it in. Yeah, it's time to start looking for a lover, and hell I may even find a husband.

I open the last confidential file on Ford's computer that he's most certainly not going to need for any of his meetings this weekend. I stand up, avoiding his stare while reaching beside his desk for my purse and the duffel bag on the floor. I packed this morning and brought my bag to work so I could leave for the airport from here.

"Any other emergencies, Mr. Ford, dial 911," I say respectively, throwing in a slight bit of humor. I sling the straps of my bags over my shoulder and step around his desk. I intend to bypass him and haul ass to the ground floor, where a taxi is scheduled to pick me up in twenty minutes.

Ford stands up before I can get past him, effectively blocking my getaway. I stop in my tracks then sidestep to the right. His long legs make him quicker at getting to the next spot on the thick, gray carpet. When he opens his arms wide, I curse under my breath. I could keep sidestepping, but I'd be doing that all day. I look toward the glass wall, but my view of the skyline is obstructed, with Mr. Ford and his file cabinet as the obstructions.

"Can I get a hug goodbye?" he asks with a frown, the timbre of his deep voice making tiny campfires blaze under every inch of my flesh.

Oh hell no, you can't say goodbye! You've said enough already, and touching me is out of the question. If I hug him, I'll probably forget how to let go, and he'll have to shake himself like a dog to get me off.

"You don't need to say goodbye, Mr. Ford. I'll be back Monday morning, not next year."

He laughs and steps forward, enveloping me in his arms anyway, making my glasses tilt sideways on my face. I reach up to adjust them, then breathe in the scent of his Burberry cologne mixed with his natural manly smell. It's a mind-scrambling concoction when he's just standing across the room, but it changes the quality of the air and makes my ability to breathe nonexistent when he's this close.

The feel of his arms wrapped around me isn't making things easy for my self-control. I'd consider him a tease, if I didn't already know that he really just wants a hug. I'm not one of the women who will ever be on the receiving end of his affection. I suspect he sees me as a little sister, and always will.

Well, at least he sees me.

Now if he would just let me go, before I wrap my arms around him, too.

"Mr. Ford," I say, my words muffled by his wide chest, my cheek resting between the ridges of his bulging pectorals.

Lord have mercy, I didn't know his chest was this big.

He rocks me just a little bit, making a rush of unwanted desire ripple through my core.

"Malisa, stay with me. I'll give you a raise."

I'd consider that too, if he was raising me from his personal assistant to his girlfriend.

"No, you've worn out the 'I'll give you a raise' line already. I have more money than I know what to do with. I'm going to Vegas, and I'm not returning until Monday." I stand firm, quietly, and in his arms, while trying not to add a meaning to his offer that he would never imply.

He releases me finally. I miss his touch instantly and rush for the door, before I change my mind about staying or the unrequited love, which refuses to go away, starts to choke me up. I deserve this break and the chance to attract everything in life that I want, which isn't going to come from him.

That's why I need this trip so badly, to find the new me that's lurking below the too big skirts, unattractive shoes, wire-rimmed glasses, and grandma blouses that I find in department stores for a steal on my way to work.

Outside, on the sidewalk in front of the glass skyscraper that's the headquarters for Ford Global Enterprises, I stand under an awning with the valet, Mikhail, who's been working here just as long as I have. While I wait for my cab, I can't help skimming my eyes over his Spanish features of long lashes, thick lips, high cheekbones, muscular build cloaked in sun-kissed skin and black uniform of suit and tie. He's handsome, but he's not Apollo.

My taxi arrives right on time. I wave goodbye to more than just Mikhail. The one-sided love I have for Ford needs to be left behind, too.

During the ride to the airport, I actually manage to stay awake until I find my first-class aisle seat on the airplane. An hour later, I hail another taxi to the hotel, where I go up to the fiftieth floor and dump my suitcases and purse on the lounge chair at the foot of the bed. I slip under a white comforter bearing the Shalimar's signature 'S.' I fall dead asleep at six o'clock in the evening, without taking in any of the sights in Sin City.

Chapter Two

My morning wakeup call arrives thirty minutes too late. I've already showered and feel completely rejuvenated after a night of uninterrupted sleep. I sit down to breakfast in my luxurious suite. For five-hundred dollars a night, it is luxuriously spacious with intricate designs, hand-carved into the Cherrywood furniture and French doors that open to the Las Vegas horizon. The bed is positioned in the middle of the room, surrounded by potted plants. It's a permanent pleasant memory etched in my mind.

However, I've admired my bedroom for the weekend enough. I have thirty minutes before my spa visit and makeover that come free with the three-room suite. Fluffy scrambled eggs, crisp bacon, coffee, and toast every morning along with my choice of dinner, whether it's French cuisine or a hamburger and fries every night, isn't a bad complimentary feature, either.

Hopefully, thirty minutes is enough time to learn how to put in the contacts that were delivered to my room before I arrived. At least, I have another year to figure out how to squeeze another eye appointment into Ford's hectic schedule that makes getting anything done for myself almost impossible.

It wouldn't be so hard if I quit my job, I think, tired of not being able to take care of myself first, second, or last. Mr. Ford has yet to figure out how to turn work off. Even when he's on his dates, I still have something pressing for his business to do. Then I go home, alone, if I find the time. *Well, not anymore dammit,* I vow, then get up from the breakfast table set at the foot of the king-sized bed with elegant posts that would touch the ceiling if it was low. Instead, it's vaulted.

After grabbing the bag with the contact lenses from the nightstand, I cross to the back of the bedroom and enter the bathroom.

I figure out how to cover my dark-brown, ordinary eyes in medicated plastic, after thirty tries for each eye. I lock the few possessions I brought with me in the suite's safe and ride the elevator down to the sixth floor.

Half a day later, I've been massaged, covered in brown and green goo from head to feet, waddled in a mud bath like a sophisticated pig, and gotten my hands and toes manicured and pedicured. The worst part of the spa was the tweezing and waxing. I made the mistake of letting Elle, the spa's beautician, have her way with my body hair. After cringing, outright yelling, and showering, while promising never to let anyone do this to me again, she gets her hands on my head of hair. I gawk at the new me covered in a robe and standing before the floor-length mirror beside her stylist booth. My hair falls down my back in a black, thick curtain of layered soft curls after a much-needed wash, condition, and trim. My skin glows. I hardly recognize myself without my glasses. I doubt if anyone else will either, including my family, which is exactly what I was aiming for.

"You like it?" Elle asks as she zips into the room with a rack of clothes. I peel my eyes away from my beautiful transformation in the mirror and turn to peruse the clothes she's selected.

"These are perfect for my body type and caramel complexion! I'm going to be a dime by the time you finish," I yell excitedly, in complete wonder at how well she has me pegged. This wardrobe will give me a much-needed overhaul.

My old clothes are comfortable, but if I want a man in my life, the granny skirts and blouses have to go.

"I think these are much more suitable for a jazzy young lady like you. You have it all sweetheart. You just need to flaunt it," Elle says and holds up a knee length skirt that looks like it will cling to every curve that I have for dear life. "Do you like this one?"

"It is gorgeous!" I say agreeing with her choice. "I just don't usually wear my clothes this tight." I'm already thinking about how the fabric will ride up on my skin.

"Well, think of it like this. If you have a man, he's going to be watching your every move, more than ever. If you don't have a man, you will definitely start to get more attention. Because honey, you have a shape that some women would die for. You might as well show it off."

Elle has made me feel good about my makeover so far. I select a couple of form-fitting dresses for the weekend, a pair of black slacks, and a royal-blue, sleeveless top for work on Monday with shoes to match from a hidden shoe rack beneath the clothes.

"Charge it all to my room," I tell Elle, "and have these sent up there for me please."

The outfit I keep, I'm going to wear while I gamble like the rest of the tourists. If I meet a guy who I'd like to take back to my room while in Vegas, well what happens here… *Hmmm.*

Elle turns away to rummage through her booth while I dress in a low-back, high-necked, fire-engine red dress. It comes to just above my knees and highlights my skin. When I twist at the waist to get a glimpse of my backside in the mirror, she starts to cluck around me like a mother hen, tugging on my clothes in places.

"You should definitely go straight to the casino to test this new look out. If it doesn't glue every eye to your body, including the straight women, come back and see me at no charge."

"Sounds good, Elle." I can tell she takes her job seriously, but I get a little worried when she pushes my boobs up with her open palms. When she stops, I'm looking at her strangely. She steps back.

"Just making sure the girls stand up, so you stand out. Your finished look is an extension of my job. You will look your best, even if I have to get down and dirty with your underwear."

I believe her and cover my mouth to keep from laughing in her face. She moves back again. Her eyes roam my body. "Damn, I'm good and you look fabulous."

"That I do, Elle, and thank you so much."

Her expression softens. Then she bends down and selects a pair of three-inch, red bottom pumps, placing them on the floor before me.

"These will go perfect with that dress."

I step into them, with Elle's help, and get a glance in the mirror at my hips being pushed out even more. She stands up to usher me into the chair again. She adds a layer of mascara, deep red lipstick, and hoop earrings and then sighs.

"All done, Malisa."

"Thank you again, Elle. I couldn't have done this without you."

"Nope, you couldn't," she fires back, before reaching for my hands and pulling me to my feet. She smiles for the first time since I arrived. "Go get 'em, girl."

"I'm going to go get something. That's for sure."

She snorts and releases my hands. I grab one of hers to leave a generous tip in it, and then I ball her hand around it tightly. She earned every dollar.

"Bye, Elle."

She pulls me into a tight embrace. "Bye yourself and don't be good," she whispers. "You're in Vegas."

I find it hard to walk away from her. She's become a friend. It's even more difficult to find an elevator that'll take me to the ground floor where the hotel's casino is. I plan to lose as little money as possible there while finding a sexy, Vegas fling.

I enter the main lobby, which has every game of chance known to man. I walk slowly into the dimly-lit, massive oval-shaped space with halogen lights on the end of long poles that extend from the ceiling over each gaming table. I have to circle around slot machines and poker tables on the outskirts of the casino before I get to the very center of the room. It's filled with people sitting around hoping to leave a little richer. There are also those that want to witness the next big win who are standing and looking over the players' shoulders.

I stop behind a crowd at the blackjack table and browse the room for an empty seat at any table in the middle of the casino. A roar follows hands flying in the air around the table behind me. I turn around to spectate, but standing five-feet-five-inches in heels, I can't penetrate or see over the packed bodies surrounding the table. I hear the crowd congratulating the winner, then most of the people leave. Before I pick one of the empty seats that are suddenly available at the blackjack table, a waitress approaches me with serving tray in hand.

"Do you want a drink, ma'am? They're free to anyone who's gambling."

I don't really want one, but every adult in the room has one.

"I'll take a long island iced tea," I tell the waitress, hoping to blend in.

"I'll be right back with your tea," she says before walking away.

I hook my heel into the low rung of an adult high chair and hoist myself up to sit down. After sliding a single hundred-dollar bill across the table to the dealer in exchange for one-dollar chips, I wait for her to flick the chips out the holder toward me and scan the table to see who's left after the big win. A man wearing a black, double-breasted suit with navy blue dress shirt and tie that looks just like the one I gave Ford two years ago for Christmas looks back. When my eyes meet familiar black eyes, which are identical to a man who's supposed to be in Utah, not Nevada, the bottom of my stomach drops. A tidal wave of anger and heat rushes me.

Why in the hell is he here?

Before I can ask why he's violating my getaway from *him* and ask myself how I managed to pick the same damn table that he's sitting at, a hand glides up my bare spine. I jerk around in my seat to see who else is violating my personal space, which I went all the way to another state to get. A dark giant of a man clothed in an aviator's brown leather jacket, stark-white dress shirt, loose fit jeans, and espresso-colored skin smiles down at me.

I take in his Caesar haircut, perfectly aligned white teeth, his build and height that matches Apollo's perfectly, and I can't look away. In a word, he's gorgeous. I'd definitely be interested in him if Ford wasn't here, but he is.

The air goes from dark and inviting to intense and awkward.

"Hello beautiful. Can I sit next to you?" The man's deep voice is just as amazing as Ford's. I imagine all of the ways I would have explored him, if Ford hadn't shown up.

"Ah… sure," I respond slowly. Words fail me the same way they did when I interviewed to be Ford's personal assistant.

I don't know how I got the job. I could barely get a word out of my mouth. Ford's presence seemed to suck the air and the intelligence right out of me. Just like now with a sexy replica of him standing beside me and Ford across the table.

The waitress returns and deposits a tall, sweating glass on the table in front of me, which is a much-needed escape from the newcomer sliding his long frame into the chair beside me. I stalk his every move, while reaching for my drink. His eyes are glued to my face.

"So how come I haven't seen you here before?" he asks coolly then sets his drink down on the green felt that lines the table.

"I'm… ah… not from around here," I stammer.

Ford's eyes drilling into the side of my face ratchets up the awkwardness a notch and adds a truckload of unbreathable tension to the air. He doesn't seem to recognize me. He hasn't said a word. Certainly, he would have spoken up if he knew it was me.

I can't seem to wrap my head around the man who's giving me all his attention while Ford, who shouldn't be here, is making it hard to inhale. I just forget about thinking clearly and take a big gulp of my drink.

"And where are you from?" ejects smoothly from the man's mouth before his long fingers wrap around his glass tumbler, distracting me from Ford's pensive stare. I glare back at him. The look in his eyes lets me know that he recognizes me and he's not happy for some reason.

"Lake City, Utah," I say coolly then turn my head to pay the man the same amount of attention that he's giving me.

My composure begins to return bit by bit. It might come back completely if I don't look at my boss, again.

The man extends his free hand to me. "I'm Derek Wilson from Pritchard, New York."

I take his warm hand and feel when Ford's stare goes frigid.

"You're a long way from home, Mr. Wilson," I mention. I'm sure Derek knows he's a long way from home, but I need this small talk as a distraction.

Derek raises my hand to his mouth and grazes my knuckles with his thick lips, making my stomach clench.

"Call me Derek, beautiful. I'm glad I'm not at home or I wouldn't have run into you. What's your name? I can't keep calling you beautiful all night." Then he cocks his head to side, appealingly. "Or I could. Your choice."

It seems Derek is a charmer and a disarmer. I laugh softly, as he probably intended for me to.

"I'm Malisa Owens, and it's nice to meet you, Derek."

I take my hand back from his, slowly.

"Malisa," Derek says my name one syllable at a time, as if he's tasting each one.

"That's me."

"So how long are you here for, Malisa?"

"Until tomorrow," Mr. Ford replies coldly, making my eyes and Derek's swivel to him.

"And you are?" Derek asks in an even colder tone.

Mr. Ford smiles and bows his head my way. "Her boss."

"Who's supposed to be in Utah getting ready for meetings tomorrow," I snipe, giving him two evil eyes. "Why *are* you here?"

He has the nerve to shrug with a small smile growing on his face like he knows he's interfering and glad of it. I grow confused. Could he want me just a little bit too?

"I decided I needed a vacation from work too. I cancelled my meetings and rescheduled them for after we fly home, Malisa."

We?

I cock one freshly arched eyebrow his way. "And you chose to come to Las Vegas where I am on your suddenly free weekend?"

"Yes. Why not? You're here already, and I can show you around the town. We could even stay until Monday if you want."

And in what capacity would I stay as lover or friend?

But I've already been work-zoned by him, I'm not about to be friend-zoned too. It's probably too much to even dream of being his lover. He has to go.

"Mr. Ford, you do know the whole point of vacation is to get away from your boss, right?"

His smile slips. "I thought it was work you were getting away from, not me."

I grind my teeth, before spitting out, "It's all the same."

He grins with one side of his mouth. "Well, I have a fun side, too."

"Oh really! What in the world made you think I wanted to see it?" Truthfully, I'd sell my first born to be *with* him when his fun side is out. "You usually reserve your *fun* side for the airhead socialites you like so much, which I'm not."

His smile grows even more crooked and smug. "Watch it, my Lisa, or I'll start to think you're jealous."

Did he just call me his Lisa?

His mispronunciation of my name throws my newly gained composure out the window and trashes my ability to respond.

"No comeback, my Lisa?" he asks, clearly goading me.

I've never known him to goad anybody. It seems Ford has much more than just a fun side. He's arrogant as hell, too. The problem with that is I don't mind it.

I reach for the long island iced tea with slightly trembling fingers, looking for Dutch courage and a way to cool the heat that floods my midsection every time he surprises me with something new about himself. I take a sip, then another, before setting my drink back down on the table. The seven different liquors on ice cool my mouth, but that's all. I'm just going to have to find the courage from within to tell him to go away.

"Mr. Ford, I'm not entertaining you tonight. This weekend was my getaway from you, but I can't make you leave the casino, so stay on your side of the table and I'll stay on mine." I turn to Derek. "I'm sorry about that. My boss doesn't have boundaries."

Derek smiles while his jet-black eyes rove over my face. "No apology necessary. I can understand why he followed you here. I would've too."

I get the nagging feeling that Derek thinks Ford and I have something going on or worse, we *had* something going on.

"No, you wouldn't understand, Derek. My boss and I only have a working relationship, and he's about to work me to death. Hence, the whole state that's supposed to be between us. The airlines allow anybody on their planes these days."

Derek laughs out loud, and the sound is just as attractive as he is.

19

Ford lets loose an alluring set of chuckles as well, which draw my eyes to his mouth just as it emits, "I came by private jet, my Lisa, and it's dangerous for you to be roaming the country by yourself. Any sort of riffraff could try to pick you up." Even his deep tenor, which can drown out a whole conference room full of bickering businessmen, can't cloak the intended insult to Derek, who stops laughing suddenly.

"Mr. Ford," I say through clenched teeth, my irritation level rising along with the heat, "it's my business who tries to pick me up. I don't show up on your dates uninvited, now do I?"

Derek chuckles quietly. "You two are like an old married couple."

I turn to glare at him. "You got that right, except there's no romance. He's more like a tyrant and an older brother, which I have one of already," I said of my brother, even though he's not biological.

Ford sits back in his chair and folds his arms. "And I take your safety just as seriously as your *man* would, my Lisa."

My man? And what is with the 'my Lisa' all of a sudden? He's not my man, and he knows I don't have one, thanks to him.

Hell, I'd have no problems with being his Lisa it if it were true, but I'm not and not going to be, so I have another sip of my drink.

Chapter Three

The dealer, a blonde woman in custom dealer's uniform of white shirt, black slacks, and black arm bands, shuffles her thin frame from one side to the other while standing inside the black jack table. "Are you going to gamble or sit here talking all night, ladies and gentlemen?"

I slide ten chips to the middle of the table so she'll shut up. Questions run through my mind like a sprinter. What boggles me the most is why Ford is suddenly being possessive? Or is my mind playing tricks on me?

I decide to go with the latter, just so I won't freak the hell out about the former. I've never seen him do possessive. I didn't think he had it in him, not where it concerns me anyway. My mind has to definitely be playing tricks on me. I wish he did have possessive feelings for me, and that's not good, so I take another sip of my drink.

The real game starts when the men ante up. That's when the losing streak begins for me. I enjoy my time with Derek, who isn't faring any better than me against the house and protesting loudly about it.

"Awe man, this game is rigged," he says and throws his hands in the air.

I roar in laughter and decide to hold off on the next hand.

Ford barely pays any attention to his cards or the dealer's, steadily sliding chips towards her. He watches me and Derek intensely as we try to get to know one each other in the noisy casino. Being closely scrutinized by the man whose eyes can be found on me at any time I look his way isn't making getting to know Derek easy.

I fidget uncomfortably under his stare and take more sips from my glass than I intend to. The drink is supposed to be for show. Now, it's the only thing keeping me calm until my chips run out. When they do, I decide this weekend is a bust for finding love or a fling, and call it a night. At least, I can catch up on my sleep.

I toss back the last of my drink, which didn't seem to have a bottom to it while I sat at the table losing horribly. I stand up, wobble on my heels, and grab for the edge of the table twice. *Dang, is it moving?*

The table had to have moved away from me the first time I reached for it. With one hand clutching the edge, I reach for the high back of the chair, making my grip on the table slip. Then I start to sway towards the chair. Derek's hand suddenly on my waist keeps me from falling against the seat that reaches my hip.

"Oh damn, I'm drunk," I mumble.

Derek's mouth tilts in one corner. "I think you need an escort to your room."

I nod, then release a nervous, uncharacteristic giggle. "I think you're right."

He stands up, while keeping me balanced.

In the corner of my eye, I see that my boss stands up, too. "I'll walk with you, Malisa. I don't want anything to happen to you on the way there." His tone is hard, his posture territorial.

I wave him off. "I'll be fine. The hotel's hallways are equipped with cameras that have security personnel behind them." I know because I checked before booking the room. I worry about my safety, too.

He grimaces. "But your room doesn't have cameras, so let's go."

Derek sets his dark sights on my boss' looming figure, which is standing rigid on the other side of the table. "I'm not a rapist or a murderer, Mr. Ford. Everything I do to a woman is consensual."

Ford grins, but it's a humorless twist of his lips. "You're not exactly going to admit to being a rapist or murderer, now are you,

Derek? And this woman is clearly intoxicated and unable to consent to anything. I'll be coming along to make sure she makes it in her room and you don't take advantage of her after you get her there."

I cringe inwardly then look up at Derek helplessly. We can't stop anyone from getting on an elevator with us or following us to my room, so there's no point in worrying about what I can't do anything about. However, I'd be lying if I said I was upset that Ford wants to make sure I get to my room safely. At least he actually cares for me, and I really don't know Derek from a can of paint.

Derek lifts one corner of his mouth in a nonchalant manner. I move away from the table and wobble on my heels again before stopping in my tracks. Derek's grip tightens around my waist, holding me in place. It feels like the earth is tilting, making me want to lean, and there's nothing right about that at all.

"That iced tea was deceptively lethal," I mention to no one in particular.

"They usually are when the waitress is refilling them when you're not looking, and you probably haven't eaten since this morning, have you?" Ford asks, but he knows the answer since I often forget to eat when at work and swamped with his pressing problems.

He's the one that always reminds me to eat.

"That means my liquor is holding me instead of the other way around, doesn't it?" I ask, before giggling again. "Oh God, why am I giggling? I don't giggle." Unless, I'm drunk that is, and I haven't been this smashed since my first and only beer in college during freshman week.

I grab a fistful of Derek's jacket before braving another step forward. When I don't lean, even though I want to, I keep moving through the casino on carefully placed heels for the wide doorway that leads through the main lobby to the elevators.

Ford grunts behind me, but keeps quiet while following us.

"Derek, what brought you to Vegas?"

Before he answers, my attention centers on the next step take I need to take. We all board the elevator and the compact atmosphere feels small because there are two giant men looking down at me from each side.

"What are you doing here, Derek? Business or pleasure?" I bring the question up again.

He laughs. "You've already asked me that, Malisa."

Oh damn! How did I become an airhead, and go from having zero men in my life to two domineering ones following me to my hotel room?

I look over at Ford. He looks absolutely delicious standing there looking protective and strong. I mentally damn him to hell. How dare he decide to follow me and block me from the only potential intimacy I've had all year?

Derek releases my waist and opens one side of his jacket with one hand. He extracts a phone from its inside pocket and extends it to me.

"Put your number in," his tone is soft and only slightly demanding. I like that about him.

Ford frowns again. "Why would she give you her number? You live in New York, and she's in Utah," he interjects.

Why does he care? He doesn't want me.

"You don't have that concern when you're dating women from different countries, Mr. Ford," I retort then take the phone from Derek.

I punch in the digits slowly. My phone is currently on my kitchen table in Utah. I should've just brought it with me. Maybe I'd have gotten the heads up when Ford decided to fly out here. I could've left before he arrived.

Chrisette Michelle's *A Couple of Forevers* begins to play in my boss' pants. That's my cell phone's ringtone and one that no heterosexual man would pick for his, which means it's *my* phone that's in his pants. I watch horrified as he unearths the singing device from his pocket, while he's wearing a guilty-as-sin look.

"Why the hell…" I start. "No forget that. *How* the hell do you have my phone?"

"When you said you didn't have it, I used the emergency key you gave me to get it from your apartment. You should have it with you at all times, Malisa. I don't just call about passwords you know. I worry if you're safe, too." He lifts the phone up in the air.

I snatch it from his hand, ignoring the niggling feeling that I'm developing. Ford wouldn't wait until now to tell me that he secretly likes me too. Would he?

I'd ask but this is something I don't want to discuss in front of Derek or anyone else for that matter because I don't know how I'll react. I'm going to get to the bottom of something else right now though.

"Gave you, Mr. Ford?" I yell, suddenly sober. "You *demanded* a key in case something happened to me. Nothing's happened to me, and giving you my key was completely unnecessary since I'm always with you. I'm *always* with you."

I'm bitter that he consumes my days and nights, while I reap no benefits. I only get heartache when he's in the same room, or out on dates. I deal with each minor or major heartbreak at his hands silently. He lives his life to the fullest with me on standby. And still, he's in the way, refusing to allow me even a few days to explore and enjoy something… anything.

And he'll keep doing this to me as long as I let him. I'm too angry to speak coherently without yelling. Yelling will just make sure he doesn't hear a word I say. I most certainly want to be heard when I give my demands to Ford.

The elevator's doors open, as if it knew I needed some space. At my hotel's room door, I spin around to face both men with my phone clenched in one of my fists at my sides. "Derek, I'll call you tomorrow to make sure you got… wherever you're going safely. I need to talk to my boss about limits. *Hard ones*," I emphasize through clenched teeth.

I have never been this angry with anyone in my life.

"Someone's in trouble," Derek mumbles then leans over and pecks me on the cheek. He whispers goodnight and walks back the way he came. I watch him walk away, along with my chances of getting laid, until he disappears into the elevator.

With my luck, he's going to find another woman who doesn't have an interfering boss following her from one state to another, nixing her chances for getting to know another man. It is beyond me why Ford is doing this when come Monday I'll still be in the work-zone of his life.

I swipe my keycard through the reader on the door angrily. After using more force than necessary to turn the handle, I have to convince myself not to stomp into the living space of my suite like a petulant child.

Ford follows me inside. When the door closes behind him with a quiet click, I turn on him in the middle of the small lane between the door and white leather couches.

"What the hell, Mr. Ford?" I ask through a gritted clench, attempting to keep my anger in check.

He steps forward, cups my face, and then his mouth is on mine. My senses scatter and my mind reels, while heat gathers in my midsection. A steady throb starts to emanate in the space between my thighs. A tingling takes over and spreads outward. When I'm feeling more than I've ever felt with any man, he steps back and smiles with one side of his mouth.

I watch speechless, as he unbuttons his jacket then tosses it behind me on the arm of the couch holding the burden of my purchases from my spa visit. His glib mood just makes me angrier.

"Call me Apollo, my Lisa," he returns to nonchalantly calling me his Lisa, like we're supposed to be here together.

It does feel like we're supposed to be together, but we're not. Being here alone with him is another mistake that my heart will pay for later. Just like accepting the job as his personal assistant was. Hindsight is always twenty-twenty. I decide that from now on I will keep as much distance as possible between us.

"First off, my name is *Ma*Lisa, not *your* Lisa, Mr. Ford." The chance for me to become anything other than his assistant has passed, or at least that's what I'm going to keep telling myself until my heart believes it. I'm done wanting something I can't have, and my heart better get used to it.

He grins. "*First off* are fighting words where I'm from, *my* Lisa."

I have no idea where he's from, oddly, and now isn't the time to ask. "Oh, we're certainly having a fight about *my* life. I've let you take too much time from it with *your* schedule and now your thinking is warped where it concerns me. That stops right now. We'll set regular hours for me to be off where you can't call, text, email, or show up as my boss. And you most definitely cannot enter my home without a valid reason! I would like my key back now."

He walks around me to take a seat on the arm of the couch across from the one wearing his jacket. I turn around to continue the fight.

"Or," he says simply then crosses his arms.

"Or I quit… right now."

He shrugs. "Okay."

Does that mean I'm fired or I can quit right now?

"Okay what?" I ask before locking my jaw, preparing to lose everything I've known and wanted, but never gotten from him.

"Okay to your demands as an employee with scheduled hours where I can't call, text, email, or show up as your boss. And, here's your key." He places my key on the table closest to him.

"Good," I say curtly then nod, unsure if I just won or lost something.

He stands up suddenly and walks toward me. My mind and mood goes on high alert. I watch him approach on silent black loafers. I step back when he invades the first of three feet in my personal space.

"What are you doing?" I ask in a whisper. "Mr. Ford…I think you should go."

His smile widens, which makes his high cheekbones lift into a predatory expression, while I back away until my spine hits the door that we both just came through. Only then does he stop, standing toe to toe with me, literally. His stare is intense enough to suck me in and make the corners of the room bend around us.

"I'm about to give you *my* demands now."

"What demands? You're not supposed to have any."

His smile grows crooked. There's no limit to what I'd give to be the woman who wakes up to that shit-eating grin every day.

Shit, Malisa, you're supposed to not be wanting him, remember? But how can I not after his lips have christened my mouth with the glories of Mr. Apollo Ford?

One of his hands lifts off, so the tip of his finger can trace the underside of my chin, making me shiver despite the heat that's made its home inside me.

"You would think that I don't have the right to have demands after I've monopolized your time for years and made sure you never met a man who would see the woman I saw beneath your plain clothes and glasses when you first walked into my office. But when you walked into the casino tonight showing off your curves and beauty, my worst fears had come true. Now, I have demands."

Chapter Four

Say what now?

It sounds like he just admitted to sabotaging my dating life so he could keep me all to himself. That can't be right. My mouth starts to open and close, wanting to speak. But my mind can't make sense of my boss' confession. Therefore, my thoughts are scattered and I'm just looking like a fish out of water.

"Could you explain in plain, small words why you monopolized my time deliberately, Mr. Ford?"

He steps closer, placing one leg between mine and killing what's left of the distance between us. Fire licks at my insides and my knees grow weak. I have to press my back into the door just to be able to keep standing upright. I force myself to concentrate on his next words and not his mouth.

"Because I wanted you for myself when we met, but you were a twenty-one-year-old fresh out of college, and just stepping into your real life. From that day forward, I considered you *my Lisa* and not Malisa. But I was twenty-eight and you weren't ready for a serious relationship yet. I had every intention of letting you do what twenty-one-year-olds should do, date, go out, live life…but I just couldn't do it."

What he shouldn't have done was made me schedule his dates so he could go out and live life, while I fell in love with him and went home alone with just my love for him as company.

"That was so fucking selfish of you and so damn unfair to me it should be criminal," I hiss.

He shakes his head and runs the pads of his thumbs across my jawline then up to my lips. Instinct makes me want to lick the fleshy pad of his finger, but I bite my bottom lip instead to keep my tongue to myself.

"No, my Lisa, I'll tell you what's criminal. The way you look when sleeping with your blouse falling open, giving me glimpses of your gorgeous breasts, and how your skirt pulls tight around your ass when you bend over my desk. I've been going through hell, trying to keep my hands off you. All of those useless dates with surface-deep women to make you jealous, in hopes that you would give me a sign, anything, to let me know you were interested, is criminal."

"I… I was… jealous," I stammer, his touch making me forget to filter my words and impossible for his words to truly sink in.

"Were you really jealous?" he asks quietly. "You never said anything."

I swallow before responding, my throat suddenly desert dry.

"Why would I? You're my boss and I'm not your type. Do I look like I want to lose my job… or you?" I question, stupidly admitting my desperation to be connected to him.

"Well, you would never lose me, and my type is the woman who doesn't know she's beautiful. She doesn't notice men who've seen the woman behind her glasses and too big clothes. That's my type. So will you have me, my Lisa?" he whispers, inciting doubts and reservations of the paralyzing kind at the same time as making my dreams a reality.

Ford has flaws that could break a woman; he's a serial dater, has never called a woman his girlfriend for as long as I've worked for him. I could lose everything I've known for four years if we rush into a relationship and my dream turns into a nightmare when he can't give me what I want the most: true love, along with a picket fence around a happy castle with kids. I haven't considered what will happen when he's had his fill of me.

Suddenly, I'm too afraid to reach out and grab what I've wanted for years. My stupid heart hadn't considered any of this before it let me fall in love with him. I didn't have to consider anything when my love was on ice, and I was convinced our working relationship would always be just that. If it's allowed to thaw completely, the consequences of sleeping with him could be catastrophic. More for me than him.

My heart starts to slowly break apart in my chest. As much as I hate the drowning feeling taking over me, maybe it just isn't meant for me to know Ford as more than my boss.

"I think getting together, even for a night, will be a bad idea, Mr. Ford," I murmur, while diverting my gaze to the thread pattern of his shirt on his chest.

"Why?" he asks in the softest of whispers above me. "You just said you wanted me."

I lick my lips, which seem to be drying out under his stare.

"I still do want you… I just don't want to be a fling of yours. Someone else's maybe, but not yours. I think you should keep dating other women. I promise it won't be a problem. I'm used to it with the countless dates I've watched you go on. That's actually helped me to manage my love for you."

His fingers slip under my chin to tilt it up and give me a front row seat to the frown he's wearing.

"Who said anything about a fling? That's not where I'm at with you, my Lisa. If you walk away from me now that I know you feel the same about me, what's going to help me manage my love for you?"

He loves me?

The slow crumbling in my chest ceases as mild shock takes over. I'm finding it hard to believe that he does after watching him go through women like sand running through an hour glass. How could he even know what love is?

"Mr. Ford, you can't love me. You've never had a girlfriend in all the years I've known you. I don't want a player. I want the whole fairytale life of king, castle, and little princes and princesses running around it. You can't give that to me because you claim to love me, but you can't see that your going out on dates with other women bothers me. I don't want to ever know how blind, insensitive, and inattentive you'd be to my feelings if we dated, because that's what you do… *date*."

He hasn't had a third date with any woman that I've had the misfortune of booking a dinner reservation for, and I don't want to join the mass of 'wined, dined, and left behind' bodies that's laying at his feet.

"Why don't you give me a chance and find out who I truly am? If I turn into all those things you think of me, then quit me."

He makes 'quitting him' sound so easy, but it's not. I'll be completely heartbroken by the time he's proven he can't be what I want. I'd rather have him in my life in a professional capacity than not at all, or I'd have quit my job and him long before now. Dating then losing him will probably break me. But losing him is what I'm afraid of the most.

"I don't want to ruin our friendship for a few moments of sex, Mr. Ford. You're not just a love interest to me. You're my employer, a damn good one that would be hard to replace, even if you're a workaholic. Plus, you're the only person I have in the way of family and friend in Utah. Much more is at stake than just my job if whatever it is you think you feel for me goes away."

And when I show up in Colorado with my tail tucked between my legs and a broken heart, my mother and father will know it. God forbid my brother, Blake, finds out about it. He'd never let me live it down. I guess it's a good thing that Blake went into the Army to pay for college a year before I left for college and never came back to Colorado.

Ford's hands glide up the side of my face to cup my ears. His eyes begin to burrow into mine, touching something deep inside me that he touches often with just a look: my soul.

"I'll tell you what's at stake, my Lisa… my heart. It's been yours since you flashed those brown eyes at me in your interview, which was the hundredth one I had to sit through of highly unqualified applicants. You were no different from everyone else that was obviously willing to learn what I needed. But I was willing to slow down and train you, so you could get used to me. I refused to ask myself why I was doing that for you, when I wouldn't do it for anyone else."

So, that's how I got the job. He wanted me too, even when I was at my most unattractive. But what did he plan to do after he gave me the job, just ignore me?

I croak, "And then?"

"After a month, when I didn't want you to go home without me, I knew what you'd done to me. I also knew if anyone else saw what I saw in you, in any way, you'd be gone for good. So yes, I stood in the way of you dating and paid you well for it. I couldn't risk losing you, even though I felt you were too young for a relationship. I had to make myself let you grow. When you threatened to quit last time, the time before now, I knew you were serious. I still couldn't bear to lose you, so I let you fly off without me."

"Then you followed me here," I murmur, falling a little deeper in love with him after his admission. How could I not when he saw past my frumpy appearance and overly thick curves to the heart of me, the woman that's been waiting for him?

At least he paid me well while I literally worked my ass off for him, losing enough weight to fit into the sleek, fitted dress the heat from his body is about to sear to my skin.

Ford leans in, his dark eyes shimmering in the blanket of darkness that's covering the living room. "Hell yes, I followed you here. I heard you asking about the best place to get a makeover while you were making your hotel reservation. I knew then my butterfly was about to come out of her cocoon and spread her wings. In no time, someone would snap you up in jar and put a lid on you. I didn't wait all this time just to lose you to someone like Derek. I came here to tell you how much I love you, for how long I have loved you, and why I've worked you until you dropped so I could watch you sleep in my home where you belong. Do you know you moan in your sleep?"

My head wobbles. "How could I know what I do when I'm passed out?"

He chuckles quietly. "Well, you do moan. It's the most beautiful sound I've ever heard, a soft and long exhale, and it's mine, so give it to me."

Holy hell! I'm stunned, unable to breathe, think, or speak.

"My Lisa," he exhales his rendition of my name like he can't hold air in his lungs any longer. What I've dreamed of has come to pass, and I'm frozen stiff and lightheaded.

Fuck! Shit! Dammit, Malisa, do something other than pass out!

His head drops, positioning his mouth only a breath away from mine. It's still too damn far away if you ask me. When he angles his head, as if he's preparing to kiss me, I have to battle with my own needs just to keep from setting my lips on his first.

"You can give me every excuse in the book, but you're mine just like that moan is. I'm not letting either go. I have waited too long to rightfully claim you both. I'll wait longer if you need more time. But I want you to do whatever amount of extra living you think you need to do, with me. Whatever concerns you have, we'll work through them."

The trace of worry and demand in his voice is too much for me to ignore. It's obvious that he wants me as much as I do him. Passing up the chance to have what I've always wanted would be stupid. My mother didn't raise a fool, and Lydia Owens doesn't tolerate them well, either.

If things go bad between us, I can always go back to managing my love and looking for a suitable replacement for him. If things get so bad my heart can't take it, I can always quit.

"Well, if you want to be mine that bad, Mr. Ford, then—" I snap my mouth shut, effectively planting my floating mind firmly in the moment.

He grins and mumbles, "Yes, I want to be yours, and more importantly I want you to be mine."

"Well, there will be no more dates with other women to make me jealous," I warn, looking up into his smoldering eyes.

"Thank God." He plants his mouth on mine, making my senses drift away, again. I have just enough awareness left to open my mouth so his thick tongue can take slow sideswipes at mine. Bolts of electricity shock my core, making it contract and release, almost painfully, and my body feel weightless. I ball my hands in the shirt material at his waist to ground myself while feeling the need to do much more than just kiss him.

I snatch my mouth off his and rest the back of my head against the door.

"Make love to me, Mr. Ford."

He drops his forehead to mine. "On one condition."

Just one?

"What… anything," I say winded, as if I've run a marathon and I'm desperate for a drop of water.

"Say my name, my Lisa."

More heat blasts through me, as if I need to be subjected to anymore fire. It steals the little air that's left in my lungs.

"I said your name already," I respond breathlessly.

"No, you called me what you always call me, Mr. Ford. Kill the professional distance between us and say my first name."

I inhale deeply then exhale, "Apollo."

He grins. My senses sharpen until I can feel the air touching down on my skin. Goosebumps raise up on my arms, and that's never happened before today. He's right about his first name; using it makes everything between us a hell of a lot more intimate. I'm sinking deeper into the love that I have for him like it's quicksand. I have no way to fight it and it may kill me.

"One day, my Lisa, I'll get you to say it along with 'I love you', but I can wait for that."

He shouldn't have to wait since it feels like I've always loved him. But, I've loved him silently for so long I don't know how to say it out loud.

"You're still bossy, even now," I gripe, with a stupid smile playing on my mouth.

Soft exhales from Apollo's opened lips begin to tickle the skin on my cheek, as quiet laughter erupts from him. "I'm bossy right now because I'm not secure in our relationship yet. That's your fault. It's your job to make sure I become secure while navigating the ins and outs of this relationship. That's if you want a king that's not blind, insensitive, and inattentive to your needs in your castle, which I'd love to buy for you someday, so our princes and princesses have a lot of room to grow... and run."

"Damn, you remembered all of that, Apollo?"

"I remember everything you say."

"So, all the late night calls for files and passwords—"

"Excuses I come up with to call you late at night," he interrupts. "Most times, I'm not even working, just thinking of you and needing to hear your voice after you've gone home."

"I thought you just liked hearing me talk when I'm drowsy," I say dryly.

He drops his head to touch the tip of his nose to mine. "I love hearing you half asleep, especially when you're in the same room with me. I took perverse pleasure in knowing I'd made you tired, even though I hadn't touched you. I've had my hands all over you in my mind."

I shudder, wishing his hands had been on more than just my mind.

"Apollo, it's perverted to work me like a dog just so you can watch me sleep."

He snickers softly, fanning my mouth with his warm, minty breath. "Yes, it is perverted. But look at it like this: I've been in love with my assistant for almost the whole time I've known her. She's seven years younger than me and doesn't know I need her more than I do air. I've suffered in the dark, alone, and in her company. All because she didn't tell me that she loved me too. Now, that's mean for you to keep your love from me. I haven't had a girlfriend since I met you, by the way. So, say the words I want to hear, my Lisa, and put me out of my misery. "

I look up at him suspiciously. He just said he was going to wait to hear those words from me. Now, he was demanding to hear them. Apollo doesn't do desperate, but he *is* doing it for me. Suddenly, I feel more secure than I've ever felt with any man.

"Guilt trips are so low for you, Apollo," I say flippantly, making him wait a little longer for what he seems to want so badly. He did make me wait for him, while he dated other people, and I'm petty enough to want some get back. "And you're not the only one who's suffered."

"I would've stopped our suffering the same month I hired you if I thought you were ready for a serious relationship."

We wouldn't have wasted so much time apart if he had, but he did what he thought was best for me. No woman can ask for more than that.

"I love you, Apollo."

"I love you too, my Lisa," he whispers, before taking my mouth with his again, sealing the deal. And if I ever lose him, my heart is done forever.

Chapter Five

Apollo steps back, suddenly breaking our lip lock and leaving me high, hot, and bothered. Before I can complain, he captures my waist in both of his huge hands and pulls me forward from the doorway then stoops down to scoop me up into his arms. His mouth is on mine again, as he turns around to walk blindly into the bedroom. He tangles his tongue with mine, then untangles it, just to do it all over again.

He squats down to lay us both on the bed, me on my back, him on his side, without breaking the kiss again. Then he slips his leg over my body, aligning his with mine and easing his weight down on me slowly and methodically. It's like he's giving me time to get used to him being this close to me. But I was used to him long before he even kissed me. My fantasies took care of that.

I spread my legs wide so his lower half can drop between my thighs, paralleling his erection with my pulsing womanhood, while he sips from the tip of my palate. It's the swipes of his tongue between the sips that stroke the deepest parts of me, leaving behind his brand on my soul, and upping the kiss from intense to mind-blowing.

The one man I dated never kissed my soul, let alone made love to it like most women wish someone would. Apollo is making it impossible to want to connect with anyone else like this, but I didn't wait this long for him to just kiss him. When I turn my head away, he groans, making me giggle.

"Apollo, take your clothes off."

"I didn't know you could be bossy, my Lisa."

"I learn from the best, and we're not in your office right now, so undress."

We really don't know each other, other than some of our likes and dislikes. If I have my way, we'll have many years to learn everything about the other. I reach for the hem of my dress that's ridden up my thighs.

"Stop," he whispers against my cheek. "I'm undressing you. I've waited too damn long for the privilege."

I move my hands away from my body, pressing them to the mattress above my head, as his tone washes over me and steals most of my right mind.

My boss loves me.

I can barely wrap my head around the thought, but his hands are expertly wrapping around my thighs where the hem of my dress lays. When he's pushed it under the globes of my ass, he drops a knee on each side of me then sits back on his heels.

"Sit up, sweetheart. I love this dress, but it has to go."

I do as I'm told, allowing him to haul the material over my head. He sucks up air loudly when he realizes I have nothing else on. He stares at my nude form while running the palms of his hands over every inch of flesh above my waist.

After he's parked his thumbs on my nipples, I reach for the buttons on his shirt. I undo them quickly and slip it off his broad shoulders. I'm feeling bold, until I get an eyeful of his washboard abs and heavily-muscled chest.

Good God!

My right hand lifts on its own. I touch the body that is about to be all mine. My fingers stroke one of his massive pectorals before skimming over the dark circle of his nipple. His chest flexes as if my touch electrocutes him, making my blood rush south to my core. An onslaught of desire sweeps through my abdomen and forces its way into the center of my thighs to press against my walls that are growing wetter with each swipe of my hand over Apollo's chest.

As much as I want to physically connect with him, I can't help fixating on it after fantasizing about it and wondering what he looked like beneath his clothes. I could've found out long before now if I had the nerve to visit him during one of his early morning workouts, but I was too chicken to view the real thing in real time. I wish I had now. Reality is way better than my dreams. My senses want to get to know everything about him.

"My pants are still on, sweetheart," Apollo mentions.

"Yes," I respond, completely distracted.

He chuckles quietly. "Are you going to take them off?"

"Yes."

My other hand drifts upwards to the neglected side of his chest. Apollo sighs dramatically above me.

"I guess I'll take them off this time, but they're your responsibility next time," he grumbles, then reaches for the buckle of his black belt, drawing my attention to the authentic Italian-leather that I ordered from Italy for his thirty-second birthday six months ago.

His full name, Apollo Sebastian Ford, is inscribed in block letters on the back side. I always thought he tossed my birthday and Christmas gifts in the back of his closet, if not in the trash, and promptly forgot about them. In exchange, he always gave me money for my birthday.

"Yes, this is the belt you bought me, sweetheart," he interrupts my thoughts. "And I love and use it like every other gift you've given me," he says, while walking backwards on his knees off the bed to stand up in front of me.

For the life of me, I can't remember the other gifts I bought him over the years, probably because Apollo is stripping down to his black briefs. They superbly frame his well-built thighs, lean hips, and the large lump that is currently pushing against the waistband of his underwear, while his slacks and shoes are pooled at his feet.

My mouth begins to water. It's as if Apollo's smooth, tan skin, only broken up by the cut of his protruding muscles, holds the only drink of water left on this earth.

"My Lisa," he calls softly to me.

I'm starting to adore the nickname he's given me. I look up. "Yeah."

"I can stand here all night if you want a full body inspection of the merchandise," he says sarcastically.

I frown. "Merchandise?" Then it dawns on me that he's actually talking about me ogling his body.

I lie back on the bed. "Inspection not necessary. I have all night to get a view of your goods."

Apollo drops down over me and catches his weight on his forearms that land on each side of my head before he crushes me.

"You have all of our lives to view the goods. I'm serious about making you mine. I'll do whatever it takes and whatever you want me to do to make that happen."

"Anything I want, huh? I love the sound of that."

He nods, his eyes dropping to my mouth.

"Take off the rest of your clothes then, Apollo. I want to see all of you."

One of his hands vanishes from his side to tug at one side of his brief's waistband, slowly. He pushes down until the tip of his erection is exposed, and then he stops to switch hands. I inhale deeply, not leaving much air for Apollo to breathe. His hand tugs at the other side of his briefs still resting on his chiseled hip, but his underwear are still holding on to his powerful thighs, as if they don't want to let go.

I lift my legs, so my toes can push his underwear down until all his clothes are on the floor where they belong. His erection springs free. Apollo's shaft is longer and wider than any other I've ever seen before. That isn't saying much, since I had a college affair with one man who took my virginity. After graduation, I moved to Utah where jobs were in abundance, without looking back.

"Thank you," Apollo says, before stepping to the edge of the bed.

My knees rock back toward my chest, giving him room to walk between them before crawling over me. Before I can say, 'You're welcome,' his lips are on mine, his tongue and penis tunneling deep inside me, inscribing his initials on every inch of soft tissue they come in contact with. I moan against his mouth, helpless as my body goes up in flames. More blistering heat that I don't need but will endure for the sake of making love with Apollo.

My bloodless fingers grab for his waist, seeking an anchor in the magical world that he's spinning around me. He withdraws almost completely from my body then drives forward, touching oversensitive spots high in my canal. I didn't think it was possible for him to penetrate me any deeper or for massive ripples of pleasure that are as sharp as a machete to streak through me without cutting me to shreds.

The walls of the dark room slip away. Apollo's thrusts pick up speed. Pressure builds in my core, and I begin to peak way too damn early. I don't usually climax this soon, or more than once during sex. I would rather go over the edge with Apollo to complete one of the many fantasies my mind has spun around him.

"Apollo, you're going to make me cum," I gasp through the storm of desire swirling within me. "I don't want to yet."

With his mouth only inches from mine, he grins above me. His body starts to pump harder, pushing me further up the steep cliff leading to bliss. I start to hyperventilate, fighting my own body for control.

"You'll cum again, I promise. Now cum for me, my Lisa," he whispers.

I go over the edge at his urging.

Apollo hammers my body for hours, sometimes shallowly so he can feast on every inch of me that his mouth can reach. When he can no longer hold back his own orgasm, he braces his weight on one hand on the mattress, begins to push balls deep inside me repeatedly. He works his fingers between our bodies. When they find the tiny nub between my thighs, six sweet strokes of his thumb is all it takes to pull another climax from me.

"Oh, Apollo!" I scream. Waves of sensation detonate in my core then scatter throughout me. Apollo collapses on top of me, trembling and sweaty, as my lungs work hard to pump air through me. "Wow," I pant into the crook of his neck.

Apollo chuckles. "Definitely."

He lifts his head, so his lips can traipse lightly over mine. "You are mine now."

Somehow, he knows a real kiss isn't possible since I'm completely out of breath.

"How the hell are you talking after that workout? I'm still trying to recover, and I didn't do any of the work."

He laughs out loud. "I exercise, remember? You don't."

I cock my head to the side. "Whose fault is that?"

"One thing at a time, love. I helped you lose the weight that you kept whining about when you thought no one was listening. I can get you in the gym, too, if you want." He sounds annoyingly smug, and I'm not psyched about that those too damn early in the morning workouts that he's so fond of.

"You *helped* me by working my ass into exhaustion, Apollo."

"No, I helped you by making sure we stayed away from the fast food chains and other salty foods that you liked. If you mentioned it, I made it happen. Anything to keep you happy."

It never occurred to me that he paid that much attention to me. Most times, I thought he was focusing on the next deal for his expanding company. I never thought the fact that he specifically requested Taziki's and other healthy foods for lunch daily was just so I would be forced to take care of myself better, by default.

"I mentioned quitting, too. Is that up for discussion?" I ask, not trying to ruin the mood, but there's the adage of 'familiarity breeds contempt' to consider. The workplace is a breeding ground for relationship troubles.

"No. I'm going to stop calling, texting, emailing, and showing up as your boss after hours, remember? I fully intend to keep that promise." I can see the hidden twist to his words a mile away.

"That's because you'll be doing all those things as my boyfriend," I deadpan.

He shakes his head. "Nope."

"No?" I ask, with my eyebrows pulling together so tightly I can feel my eyes crossing.

Apollo rolls off my body to lie on his side beside me. He props his head up with a hand. He looks down at me with a deeply intense look on his face meant to pierce through the top layer of my eyes. Even if that isn't what he means to do, that's what he's doing, anyway.

"No, my Lisa. I'm too old to be someone's boyfriend. I want to be your man, one day your fiancé, but always the maker of all your dreams coming true. I want everyone to know I love you and I'm your best friend who'll blindly follow wherever you go, because even one minute without you is too many. That's why I'm here. I couldn't make it an entire weekend without you."

I grin stupidly, hanging onto his every word. He steals my sanity whenever he speaks.

"Okay, you're my man then."

His fingers trespass against my erect nipple. He squeezes it between his index finger and thumb. A bolt of lightning streaks downward to my core and electrocutes it. I close my eyes to concentrate on what his touch is doing to me, memorizing it.

"So, what are you going to tell Derek when he calls you?" Apollo asks casually, as if he isn't flipping my body inside out with just his touch.

I squeeze my thighs together to contain the onslaught of sensations barreling through me.

"What do you want me to say?"

He twists his head propped up on his hand just as I open my eyes.

"Fuck off would be good."

I begin to giggle wildly. "That's just rude."

"Exactly and Derek will get the message that you're mine."

"What if he only wants to be friends?"

Apollo grimaces and stops fiddling with my breast to make intense eye to eye contact.

"Please! He damn near ran over to you tonight, then touched you to warn off the other men headed in your direction. Being friends with you is the least of his intentions, but he can't have you."

His head drops, so he can plant a noisy kiss on my mouth.

"You sound so freakishly possessive, Apollo." And it sounds damn good too, after pining for him for as long as I have.

"I am possessive. I'd welcome the same emotion from you. I wish that I was exaggerating about Derek, but you're beautiful, and you always have been."

A well of emotions overflow into my throat. I have to swallow them down and distract myself by running a fingertip across his chest from top to bottom, where his pectoral meets the mattress.

"So, you want me to be visibly upset when beautiful female clients come into the office?" I don't think he's considered just how bad that can get, and it's why I'm so against working with him while dating him.

He squeezes my nipple, again.

"Not so upset that it interferes with the money we'll need to buy your castle, but you could drape a hand on my shoulder during meetings if that makes you feel better. It won't hurt anything. Or you can smile at me from time to time to let everyone, including me, know who I belong to. You never do any of those things, and I could never prove if you cared for me as much as I do you."

I shift closer to him.

"Oh, I cared too much. I don't know how you missed my snippy moments whenever you asked me to make dinner reservations for you plus one. But as far as our castle, we'll buy it together."

He shrugs and chuckles low in his throat.

"You get snippy anytime you're tired. How was I to know the difference? I'm sorry if I ever hurt you."

"You couldn't tell the difference because you never let me sleep!" I yell then slap at his chest. "I'm always tired."

His head dips closer to mine until his mouth is close enough to be thoroughly kissed.

"I never let you sleep because I can't sleep without you, my Lisa. I sure as hell wasn't going to run you off by asking you to sleep in my bed with me...or yours. It wouldn't haven't mattered to me. You spoiled me with those moans of yours. Now, I'm addicted and can't sleep without hearing at least one before I go to sleep."

More emotions threaten to strangle me. I'm elated that he truly loves me, but his mention of sleep incites the urge to yawn.

"As much as I love talking to you, love, I have this boss who works me around the clock. Tonight, he worked me into overtime, and then past it, even while I'm on vacation."

Apollo's lips lower to mine then give more than they take with slow caresses and firm presses, as if he's treasuring the contact between us. Another yawn rises. To keep from yawning into his mouth, rudely, I snatch my head away and cover my mouth.

He chuckles quietly above me. "Turn over and sleep, love. I'll see you in the morning."

I shift to my side until my front is pressed to his front, my cheek against his chest. He slips his arm beneath mine, places his hand against my spine, and pulls me even closer, where I've longed to be. Sometimes, I can't even remember when I didn't wish for this. The rhythmic rise and fall of Apollo's chest provides the perfect relaxing setting for sleep to overtake me.

Chapter Six

Heat imbeds itself under every inch of my skin and teases the edges of my sleep, until I peel back my eyelids. I have to shut them back. The French doors allow the sun to shine brightly in the room. More heat wafts from the hard body and arms that I'm cocooned in.

I smile. Even in his sleep, Apollo is possessive.

"Is that smile for me?" he asks from behind me.

I twist in his arms to face him. His head is propped on one hand. Combine the heat from his body and stare, and who needs the sun?

"No, I'm not smiling for you, but because of you," I confess.

He grins. "I think that's even better."

"Did you sleep at all? I know you're an insomniac."

He shrugs with one shoulder. "I slept a few hours, then woke up to one of your moans. I laid awake hoping for another one."

That is troubling to me. He needed to sleep.

"Apollo, you need to get more rest. It's not good to work like do with just a few hours in between for sleep."

He shifts on the bed, scooting downward until his face is level with mine on the pillow. "Can I assign making sure I get sufficient rest to one of your duties?"

"I'd think you was joking, but I have the feeling you're not," I respond dryly.

"No, I'm not. I've never felt so rested than when I'm with you, however long I sleep."

"Okay. What makes you sleepy?"

"Reading contracts," he says.

"Then you will read a contract every night at a certain time until we train your body to get tired at that hour."

"Won't work."

He couldn't have possibly even given my suggestion a thought before responding.

"Why not?"

"Because I need one of your moans…after I've had you, and/or while I'm having you. Your choice."

"Your way could work, too," I agree, trying hard to hide the absolute joy that's traveling through every part of me. It's hard to believe that he craves me as much as I do him.

Me. Not the sophisticated socialites he normally dates, and it's mind-blowing.

Apollo's fingers begin walking up the bare skin of my side. "Can't it work now?"

I sigh, content. "Sure, but only if you let me use the bathroom first."

"Ummm… not yet."

"My bladder is full and I need to brush my teeth," I admit.

He rolls over, forcing me onto my back.

"Afterwards," he murmurs.

I part my legs to give him room inside them. I wrap them around his back. Though I'm not crazy about morning breath, I allow him to seal our mouths together in an airtight kiss, while he teases the opening of my body with the tip of his penis, working me into a heated, wet state. I'm not quite prepared for when he bottoms out inside me, filling me to capacity. But there's nothing uncomfortable about the feeling of being full of him. Deeply seated in my canal that fits snugly around his base, it's as if our bodies are made for one another.

When he begins to move in and out of me with ease, the room folds away, again. It's just him and me moving up through the heavens. Nothing else exists. Even in my fantasies, I've never dreamed of this place, and I feel cheated.

Apollo snatches his mouth away from mine suddenly. His pace quickens along with his breathing. My heartbeat keeps in time with his rapid and shallow inhales and exhales, until I slip over the edge, dragging him groaning and quivering with me. This climax seems so much stronger than last night. I tumble through the clouds like a runaway train, with the blunt edge of my nails digging into his shoulders.

"God, Apollo!" I yell, needing the orgasm to fade already. There's only so much pleasure a body can take.

"If that's what you want me to be, sweetheart," he grunts above me then settles on top of me finally. His head lays on my breasts, and his arms wrap tightly around me. His chest heaves against my abdomen filling up with my humor.

"You are absolutely conceited, Apollo," I say breathlessly.

His lips curve against my stomach. "I don't know how you missed that for this long. You came harder, didn't you?" he asks winded, staring off into the bathroom.

I simply nod.

He lifts his head. "That's because your bladder is full. Don't ask me to go into detail. It's just something I read somewhere."

"I wouldn't ask anyway. No air."

He rolls to the empty side of the bed. "I can't breathe either, and, strangely, I think I need a nap."

I sit up beside him. I'm invigorated though I can't breathe properly. I guess love has that effect on me.

"Then sleep. I need to shop for some outfits to take back home."

"Can I take you out tonight?" he asks, while I slide to the edge of the bed. "I don't want to take you home yet. I like this place. You told me that you loved me here."

I glance back and have to swallow my rising emotions, again. They're not only threatening to choke me but make me misty-eyed as well.

"Yes, we can go out. What do you want to do?"

"I'll take you to dinner first then we can play tourist to walk off our meal, so wear comfortable shoes. Then we'll come back here and do whatever you want."

I smile. I didn't think I'd ever hear those words out of his mouth. 'Whatever' definitely covers the complete list of things that I'd like to do with Apollo in bed. Out of it. On the sofa. In the shower. The balcony. Like I said, a whole range of things.

He narrows his eyes at me.

"What's the smile for, my Lisa?" he asks warily, intruding on my X-rated thoughts.

"Just thinking about what 'whatever' could mean."

His chest begins to vibrate with his rising hilarity. "Why do I think I just opened a bag that I may not be able to close back?"

I slip from the bed to walk toward the bathroom, stopping in the doorway to glance back. "You may not want to close it back."

Before I'm tempted to forego the shopping and give him a glimpse into the bag of my fantasies, I close myself off in the bathroom to take a shower. I'm risking having to go to work naked on Tuesday if I decide to give him a sneak peek. Tonight will have to do for checking things off my mental list of ways to screw Apollo's brains out. God knows I'm not a prude, just went without intimacy for too long. I may not sleep around, but I'm not meant to be alone, either.

When I come out of the bathroom, Apollo is asleep on his back with my pillow thrown across his chest. The early morning rays flooding the room highlight every inch of his handsome face. Sleep makes the chiseled planes of it so much softer. I stand at the side of the bed, studying his features. I imagine him as the typical popular teenager beating back the girls with a stick. Or maybe he didn't.

Sometimes, I think he jumped straight out of his mother's womb dressed in Armani with a contract in his hands, which reminds me that I've never met his parents. He's never mentioned them. There is so much more to this man that I failed to learn. I have some serious catching up to do.

At least I have an excuse for being behind the curve; I used most of my brain power to hide my love from him and everybody else in the office. Jenna, his secretary, is extremely nosy, when it comes to Apollo's love life. She's not so proficient in making sure his contracts are error proof though. He has no problems with asking me to check behind her for mistakes, as well as other employees, adding supervising their work to my long lists of responsibilities.

It was always easier to just do the work than complain about it, which means I carry half the blame for working around the clock. This has to stop, even if Apollo and I are a couple now.

Who will be around each other day and night...

The kiss of death to any relationship.

I still need to quit my job.

I don't have to be a rocket scientist to know that Apollo isn't going to do well with me changing jobs. But I'd rather have him in my world for years to come than us squabbling in the office, eventually breaking up because we don't have space to miss each other. If he truly loves me, he'll understand. I just hope I don't ruin the night when I bring this subject up.

I walk quietly away from the bed to the living room, where I left the extra outfits from the spa. In the top garment bag is the other dress I bought. It's white and form-fitting with thin straps, tight bodice and a scoop neckline that's supposed to serve as a bra. I step into it. The bodice pushes up my breasts, making them look like they're going to pop out of the top at any given minute.

The attached pencil skirt molds to my hips, ending mid-thigh. I add the strappy, white heels to my feet, which I brought along with the dress. I stroll quietly into the bedroom to retrieve my purse from the lounge chair and the keycard from beneath the dress laying in a puddle on the floor.

I pick it up and toss it onto the chair then stop beside the bed again. I look down on Apollo and want to kiss him goodbye. But he's a light sleeper who needs all the rest he can get. I begin to wonder if I leave my position would he get any sleep at all, or anything done at work. He doesn't have the most dependable employees. They seem to sense when they can slack off on their jobs and take full advantage. That was fine when Apollo focused much of his time on keeping me close and I didn't know any better. Now that I'm the one staying close to him, maybe he'll make *all* his employees earn their checks.

At least, I hope so.

I settle for blowing a kiss goodbye over his sleeping form. I leave the suite and ride the elevator to the ground floor. I ask the same desk clerk from last night, Liam, if he knows where a reasonable shopping center is. He walks outside and hails a taxi being driven by a man dressed in full African attire. Liam directs him to take me to a shopping center five miles away, while I climb in the backseat. Twenty minutes later, we sit in front of designer stores, the likes of Saks Fifth Avenue and Prada.

"Could we find a mall?" I ask from the backseat.

The driver turns around in his seat. "I take you somewhere better two miles back other way. My sister works at outlet store for these places. Way cheaper," he says in broken English and a heavy accent.

After ten more minutes in crawling traffic, we arrive at the outlet store that's much bigger than the designer stores. I pay him an ridiculous fee for a seven-mile trip, before getting out in front of double glass doors with display signs for the same designer gear I refused to buy up the street. I get out the car and go inside.

The hours slip away, as I browse overstuffed, circular clothes racks and shoe displays climbing to the ceiling on both sides of the short cashier counter at the back wall. After amassing a stockpile of clothes for every type of occasion and leaving my choices with a cashier, I get in the long line with other customers waiting to pay. My cell phone rings in my purse. When I see Mr. Ford blinking across my display screen, I swipe the accept icon, hurriedly.

"Hi."

"Hi yourself," he replies in a deep drawl that skips down my spine. "Now, where are you?"

"I'm in an outlet store three miles away from the hotel, and I hope they deliver because I think I bought half the store. Considering the baggage fee that I'll be charged at the airport, I'll come out better having it all shipped home."

"Tell me what store you're in and I'll come pick you up."

As much as I love that he cares, I'm a big girl who loves her independence.

"Thank you, Apollo. But I can get back to the hotel with my bags...one way or the other."

"I know that, but I'm missing you, and I want to see you as soon as possible. Don't worry about your bags. My jet can haul all that you buy." His tone deepens, and my heart flutters even though I have to refuse his offers.

"I flew here commercial, sweetheart, and the airlines won't refund half of my round-trip ticket if I only use half of it."

"You didn't pay for your ticket, baby."

What the hell does he mean I didn't pay for my ticket?

A mild case of shock descends upon me. "You mean I flew free?"

He laughs. "Something like that."

The line moves up one person while I try to make sense of his vague explanation. I step forward, utterly confused and unhappy about possibly being arrested for stowing away on a plane as soon as I get to the airport's checkout counter.

"Either I paid for my ticket or I didn't, Apollo," I whisper, while looking around, suddenly paranoid. "Which is it?"

"You didn't."

My heart sinks into my stomach, rendering me unable to speak.

"Oh God," I moan quietly into the line.

He starts to laugh. "*I* paid for everything you wanted, my Lisa. Your ticket, contacts, suite, spa visit, clothes, and I'll pay for the ones you're about to get now when I find you."

No longer paranoid, I feel shanghaied and angry. He hadn't checked with me first before shelling out his money. I wasn't raised to let anyone give me anything, giving them the opportunity to demand something in return that I'm not willing to give.

"Why didn't you tell me, or at least ask if I wanted you to pay for my trip, Apollo? I'm not a prostitute—"

"I'm not your john either," he interrupts, in a cold tone.

"As I was saying, I'm not a prostitute, and I can buy my own things," I hiss, keeping my voice low and our first argument out the ears of the customers around me. "That's why I work every freaking day for you, Apollo."

He groans loudly. "Of course you're not a prostitute, or you wouldn't be my assistant. But when a man loves a woman, he pays for the things that she wants and needs because it's the sole reason why a man works—to provide. And you wouldn't know I'd paid for anything if I didn't want you to fly home with me and not worry about blowing your money."

The phone line begins to crackle between us.

"My Lisa," he calls out, as if he's afraid I've hung up.

His voice echoes in my ear, which only happens when both phones in use are in close proximity of each other. A sharp tingle develops between my shoulder blades. I recognize it as the eerie feeling that comes from being watched. I turn around to find the customers behind me are looking back at Apollo. He's standing at the entrance several yards away. Both of his piercing black eyes are trained on me.

Oh my damn! He's here.

Chapter Seven

My hand slowly lowers the phone to my side. Suddenly, the atmosphere is too thick to inhale. Apollo's so damn beautiful in his tailored black suit it almost hurts to look at him. How did he become more handsome than he already was?

I'm still mad with him for taking the liberty to throw his money around before asking if it was okay with me. Of course, I would've told him no. I don't want a man taking care of me. What happens when he can't or doesn't want to take care of me anymore?

I don't know, and I never want to find out.

I turn completely around, giving him my undivided attention. The lady standing in front of me glances over my shoulder then signals with a nod of her head for me to back up. I realize the line has moved and take two mini-steps back, refusing to break eye contact until he says something or comes to me… anything to give me the idea that he understands why I'm angry and we've made it through our first argument.

When the lady signals for me to move again, I accept that he isn't going to *do* anything and turn around to face the front. Apollo materializes beside me, almost instantly. I breathe out, consumed with relief, but the customers are weirdly silent after all the chatter I'd ignored during my shopping spree. The silence becomes too loud to endure. I start to count the people waiting in front of me, while sneaking sideways glances at Apollo. He's staring straight ahead.

Finally, the line dwindles down to my turn to check out. The salesgirl that I left my selections with hauls them on the countertop beside her register. I wait for what seems like forever for her to scan the barcodes and bag my purchases. The tension mounting between Apollo and I grows by leaps and bounds. The whole store seems to be waiting right along with me for one of us to say something. I can't think of one thing to say that won't ignite the tension into a full-blown argument complete with yelling, so I stay silent.

The quiet is broken by the sales clerk who tells me my total. I give her my credit card. She swipes it quickly then hands it back, along with the receipt for me to sign. Apollo begins collecting the bags. I look up at him, then at the bags. He returns my look with the sharp penetrating stare that he usually reserves for those who have crossed the line with him.

How can wanting to be my own woman and pay my own way cross a line?

It feels like he's drawing that line in the sand as he looks down at me.

"Can I get the bags, Malisa, or do you want to carry them, too?" he snipes at me, while pronouncing my name correctly.

I'd already grown to love his alteration of it.

Shit! He's angry. This is not *good.*

When Apollo's this angry, he can become an opponent on a battle field in a war that no one wants a part of. I never wanted to be the one on the opposing side either. It's reserved for the losers that make the mistake of going up against him.

We need some space before one of us says something else that we'll both regret. I'm already regretting going off on him about spending his money on me. I don't want my regrets to grow.

"Well, I can get them, Apollo, because I think—" The ability to speak fades away, when he sets the bags down on the counter gently, as if he's releasing me, too.

I slip into major heartbreak territory. I have been here many times before because of him, so it's not something that overly concerns me. When he turns to face me, holding himself stiffly and a canyon's width apart from me mentally while towering over me, that does worry me. I look away long enough to give the clerk the signed receipt back.

"Do you want to make your way back to the hotel, too?" he asks, too calmly for my liking.

My eyes snap to his, which are snapping back at me. I'd hurt him without meaning to, and he's being a gentleman about it, which only makes me feel so much worse. He's taking my refusal for help with the bags the wrong way, too.

I just want both of us to have time apart to cool down. The height of our emotions will lead to yet another argument, where we won't hear a thing the other says. Our fragile beginning can't afford that. I'm not going to explain why I am the way I am in front of an audience, either. Though none of the customers seem to mind the drama bonus added to their shopping spree.

We need to get out of this store, and fast.

"Apollo—"

"Well?" he cuts in belligerently. "Are you getting back to the hotel on your own or not?"

I step back from the quiet anger rippling off him in thick waves too big to inhale.

"I…" I stammer and have to swallow. "I probably should, Apollo. You're upset." And I sure as hell don't want this to be our last fight.

His chest begins to rock with sarcastic chuckles emitting low from his throat.

"Upset is the tip of the iceberg, Malisa, but I'll get out of your way."

"Apollo—"

He turns on the heels of his Italian loafers and walks away. I don't have to worry about us not hearing one another. He's not even letting me get a word in to explain that he's anything but in my way. My feet stick to the floor, the shock and fear of losing Apollo proving too heavy to move. I, and everyone else in the store, watch him leave. When the glass doors automatically open for him then close behind him, the customers start to talk amongst themselves. The different opinions spur me to take my leave.

Only one person's opinion matters to me, and he's already walked out the door.

I grab the sacks off the countertop, one by one, sliding the thin, paper handles of as many as I can along my arms before collecting the rest in my hands. I rush toward the exit, hoping the man I love hasn't actually left me behind. When I get outside in the cool, late morning air, I realize I'd forgotten to do my due diligence and ask the salesgirl for a number to the local taxi company, just in case I can't find Apollo. Taking care of myself is why Apollo and I are at odds, and yet, I'm already forgetting to do it. I look around the parking lot. He's nowhere to be seen.

There aren't any idling cars or limos from the local car service waiting in the colossal lot. I could go back inside the store to ask the sales clerk for a taxi's service number, in front of the mob that had been privy to the fastest breakdown of a relationship before it could even leave the state it began in.

I'd rather hoof it back to the hotel first.

Mercifully, a yellow cab turns into the parking lot, circles it, and stops in front of me standing on the sidewalk like a lost orphan. The passenger window rolls down, before I can step off the curb. An older white man leans over his passenger's seat and peers out of the car, with a brown tweed gentleman's cap tilted to the side.

"Are you Malisa Owens?"

I nod, stunned. Only Apollo would know my full name in all of Nevada and Utah. Because of my job, I have no friends anywhere to speak of anymore.

The man shifts back to the driver's seat then opens his door. I wait for him to open the back door for me. It's impossible for me to do it with all the bags in my hands. I push my way inside the car behind the mountain of sacks, regretting the shopping that started this mess between Apollo and me.

When the driver's back in his seat, I gratefully grumble, "Thank you."

Now why couldn't I just say that to Apollo? Because he's not a taxi driver that I'll pay for his help at the end of his service, and I'm an idiot who had it drummed into me to stand on my own two feet by my parents.

Somewhere along the way, I'd forgotten to be grateful when receiving a gift of any kind from anyone, and that people helping me have to be willing to help in the first place. That's a gift, too, whether I'm paying for their service or not.

Pure misery swoops down on me. I lift my hand to swipe my suddenly aching forehead, but the damn sacks get in the way of even that. I can only blame myself if I've lost the man who I've dreamed about, wished for, and finally gotten.

And he's probably cancelled our extended vacation by now.

There's only two things left for me to do: apologize to Apollo and use the other half of my ticket. Yeah, I don't think so. I'll be buying another ticket home. Apollo's certainly dumped my ass along with the extended vacation, and there's no point in using the other half of the plane ticket he bought, since I was too stubborn to graciously accept the first half.

So stupid, Malisa! Apollo's pissed. He'll be easier to talk to... oh, in about a week, or a year.

However long it takes, I'll wait. But I won't even think about how he thought enough of me, even while angry, to secure a ride for me back to the hotel. I'll only make myself feel worse if I do think about it, if feeling worse is even possible.

The cab arrives in front of the hotel. I dread going inside, afraid I'll run into Mr. Ford leaving, Apollo a thing of my past now. That's my fault too. I'd ignored my concerns about us going to the next level in our relationship, like an idiot, and look what happened. Still, I square my shoulders and find the strength to face him, anyway. It's going to happen, today or tomorrow. Either way, I had to get it over with and maybe even find a way to move on, because I have no proof that he hasn't already.

I just don't know if moving on is possible when I'd finally gotten where I wanted to be, in his arms.

I release the bags in my hand to reach into my wallet clutched in the other hand that's still loaded down with bags, intending to pay for the ride.

The driver looks back and shakes his head. "The man already paid me and told me to tell you that he'll see you Tuesday morning."

My mouth drops open, weighted down with pure shock. Apollo hadn't cancelled anything but us.

"Tuesday!" I shriek, panicking. "What happened to 'he can't sleep unless I'm there'? He needs to hear me moan before he can! Did he just leave because I didn't want him spending money on me? Now he doesn't even want me in the office Monday?"

I've sunk low, resorting to taking my frustrations out on the innocent driver who doesn't know me or Mr. Ford. But Apollo banning me from the office until Tuesday is pure overkill, or at least that's what I think.

The driver shrugs, his mouth drooping at the corner. "I don't know. I was just told to deliver you and the message here. That's it, ma'am."

I wait for the beating of my heart to resume its normal pace and my emotions to settle. Neither happens, and it's probably not going to until I'm somewhere quiet and have had time to process what just happened. That isn't going to happen while I'm sitting in the cab, probably not in the near future either. It looks like I'm going to need my own two feet, after all. So why do my legs feel wobbly and I'm sitting down?

Stop asking questions you know the answers to, Malisa, and get out the damn car!

"Fine," I grumble beneath my breath. "If he doesn't want me around, I won't come around."

I begin to collect the bags gone astray on the backseat. The driver gets out the car. When he opens my door, I step out onto the curb, clumsily.

"Thank you," I say, before hauling myself behind the bags out the car.

A young man in a bellhop's uniform appears out of nowhere just as I step in front of the lobby's door. When they slide open, I shake my head, refusing his help and locate the elevator.

As it rises to my floor, my mind whirls in circles, determined to work out what to do next. I'd planned to go home and apologize to Apollo for going overboard with my independence. Yes, I recognize the error or my ways, so sue me for being human.

But what's the point of apologizing, when he doesn't even want me in the same space?

My heart isn't going to just let me work with him and not be with him, not after getting a taste of an exceptional man. I guess I should keep my heart and my ass out of Apollo's space and life altogether for a while.

At least, I had a perfect early night and late morning with the love of my life before things went south, the very thing I was afraid would happen; my friend, my secret love, and my job all gone in one swoop.

The elevator doors open. I step out into the long corridor, and turn toward my hotel's door. It dawns on me that Apollo is really gone, and he isn't coming back. A steady throb begins in my chest. My eyes and nose burn. Incoming tears tighten my throat, making it almost impossible to breathe.

What's the point of being independent, Malisa, if you break down at the first sign of trouble because your stupid heart is codependent on Apollo?

And I'm certainly going to come apart at the seams, right here in the middle of the hallway, but I'll be damned if I do it for everyone to see.

I hold myself together long enough to open my door, drop the sacks on the living room floor, with no care for the few breakables that I'd bought as gifts for my family. I walk blinded by tears to the bedroom. I turn my cell off and disconnect the hotel's phone from its base. The only left do is collapse on the bed and cry. Watching Apollo go on dates has nothing on watching him leave me behind then telling me to stay away.

When the tears let up, I make a pact with myself.

Come hell or high water, I'll find a way to get over Apollo. This has to be why my parents told me countless times to make my own way in the world. Shit always hits the fan at some point, and I need to be able to shield myself until someone unplugs the fan, or it runs out of disgusting things to throw at me.

My heart is being pummeled from the inside out. I'm being rained down on with memories of Apollo, which are attached to this room that I've made my sanctuary. I don't want to be let out of it either.

Eventually, sleep finds and abandons me. Monday morning's arrival is reflecting too brightly off the French doors' glass into my eyes, which are puffy and sore from crying most of Sunday. Despite the promise I made myself, I don't feel like standing on my own two feet for any length of time. After only one night with Apollo, my heart isn't the only thing codependent on him. I miss his warm body next to mine, his gentle yet searing touch on my skin, and his deep voice that sends shivers down my spine for no reason at all.

Why did I ever let us go beyond professional?

Now, I've lost everything over money, *his* money. It's the very reason we'd met in the first place. I needed it so I could stand on my own two feet. Yet, I essentially punished him, and me too, for it.

I can't stay here all day crying about it though, so I sit up slowly. My body is not even remotely interested in actually getting up. More tears slip from my eyes, when I should be all cried out, or at least dehydrated. I swipe at them angrily.

Dammit, Malisa, the damage is done now! You can't keep crying over spilled milk.

Except, I can't stop crying, and need one more day to get it out of my system.

Chapter Eight

Tuesday morning creeps into my existence, cloudy, gloomy and gray, as if it's afraid to come anywhere near me. That's probably because it's finding me not much better off than I was yesterday. My legs are still wobbly. I slide to the edge of the bed and pick up the hotel's phone. I call the front desk and request another night's stay. First, I get a much too damn chirper female.

"I'll be happy to charge Mr. Ford's card for another $2500, Ms. Owens."

I gasp and clutch the cord of the phone, wrapping my fingers around it tightly, damn near strangling it.

"Wait. I thought the room was five hundred a night!" I didn't mean to yell rudely in the clerk's ear, well, actually, I did. I must have been given Apollo's room by mistake.

"No ma'am, our suites start at fifteen hundred. The *standard* rooms start at five hundred."

"I'm supposed to *be* in a standard room," I inform her.

"No ma'am, we got a call to…" I tune her out, realizing what's happened. Apollo upgraded my room before I got here, spent ten thousand dollars for a weekend and extended stay, and then left me here alone to cry over him.

Is he out of his damn mind? Probably not, but he's out of a whole lot of money, and he's probably not going to let me repay him.

"Ms. Owens," the clerk calls out worriedly.

"Never mind, I'm checking out and I don't need a bellhop."

I hang up on the woman and make myself take a quick shower, before putting on the outfit that was supposed to be for Monday. I'm packing up to go home, but not the one I've made in Utah. I need familiar, loving arms around me, and the space to reset. That can only be found in Colorado.

Apollo's arms and space isn't an option. I'm not stable enough to not break down in his presence when I look at him. Since he left, a storm of my emotions seem to be brewing just below the surface of my skin.

Normally, I'd order breakfast before leaving a fancy hotel like this. I'm not a girl who's afraid to eat, but my appetite has been nonexistent since Sunday. A lot of other things left with Apollo, too (I mean Mr. Ford) like my courage to return to Utah and face him. I just can't bring myself to do it, yet.

Maybe, I should just quit my job now. It's been a long time coming anyway, and I should've done it a long time ago. I'd have a whole heart to give to someone else if I had, and could've skipped this sorry state that he's left me in. To know he once loved me only makes the constant ache in my chest worse and my legs even wobblier than before.

I slump down on the edge of the lounge chair at the end of the bed and rub the side of my chest that's housing the dull pain with the heel of my hand. My eyes settle on the desk along with a computer sitting across the room against the wall. I get an idea. Since I'm a damn coward who can no longer stand on her own two feet, I can email my resignation letter to Mr. Ford, with a sincere apology for not giving two weeks' notice and a brief explanation at the end. I think it's best for everyone involved if I make a clean break from Global Ford Enterprises. He can toss my belongings in the trash. Everything there will just remind me of Apollo, anyway. Most of the personal photos on my desk can be replaced with a call to my mother.

But my conscience has a tough time with just letting go of my irreplaceable possessions made with love. While I'm being a coward, why don't I just pack it all in? Have a shipping company pack up my apartment and deliver everything to the closest storage facility, and then go backpacking in the next country, while hoping Apollo forgets all about the breach of the employee five-year contract that I'll commit. It doesn't end for another nine months.

I sit straight up on the lounge and groan, "Shit! The contract!"

I'd like to think that Apollo wouldn't be so cruel as to make me finish it to the end of term, but I know he will. He has yet to let *anyone* out of a contract that Global Ford Enterprises benefits from. I still need some time to get myself together though, and I have weeks of vacation time that I never took. A few more days without me in his space shouldn't hurt.

I gather my bags, all of them, and leave the room. I don't want to go. This is where he told me he loved me and would never let me go. How did that change in less than twenty-four hours?

Maybe it was all a dream, I think, as I struggle with my bags onto the elevator until the doors close behind me. I stand with my back to them, huffing and puffing, trapped between the doors and the sacks, unable to turn around. I should have requested a bellhop instead of refusing one. The independent life is not all it's caked up to be.

I imagine that this is all a dream that turned into a nightmare when I left Apollo sleeping Sunday morning. But if it was all a dream, I can just forget it all ever happened and stop mourning the loss of my king, right? Maybe the world is flat with four corners, too. If I can make myself believe that, I can believe anything.

"I'm in deep trouble," I murmur to the compartment, "and up to my neck in it."

When the elevator arrives at the ground floor, I reverse out of it and approach the same bubbly clerk who unknowingly clued me in on Apollo upgrading my room. She's even happier to call me a cab. My first stop is the local post office, where I have my bags one-day expressed to my parents' house and avoid the legal stickup for a baggage fee at the airport, which is my last stop before Colorado. After purchasing a round-trip ticket to my hometown, Arrow, I leave the

69

half-used round trip ticket at the counter. It's symbolic; I'm leaving Apollo behind like he left me. Well, it's symbolic in my mind at least.

Yeah, that worked so well on Friday, didn't it? I internally curse symbolism. I didn't know he loved me then. Now, I have an hour's flight to convince to my heart to leave that love behind. I spend most of it trying not cry in front of the other passengers and wishing for things that I have to wait for. By the last leg of the journey, I know I haven't fooled the person sitting next to me in the aisle seat at all, a little old lady who keeps looking at me sideways. I smile weakly whenever I catch her doing it, then go right back to wishing I was already home with my parents who undoubtedly will hover like helicopters.

I'm their only biological child, so their attention can get smothering, and their advice comes in bushels. I need all of that right now, without giving away the state of my love life. If I had at least one girlfriend, I could confide in her before I got home, but I'm paying the price for letting Apollo… dammit, I mean letting *Mr. Ford* monopolize my time. Now, I'm in danger of disappointing my parents if they ever find out why I haven't come to visit in years.

I guess they better not find out then.

The plane finally touches down. When I've offloaded myself into the airport that's fifteen miles away from Arrow, I turn my phone back on and join the queue for a rental car. I'm not going to be picky. Anything with a four-wheel drive and snow chains will be fine since Colorado is beginning its winter and tourist season. It comes with fast-approaching blizzards and the freaky snowstorms that appear out of nowhere.

My phone begins vibrating with back-to-back calls and texts. I'd turned it off for Sunday night to Tuesday morning's crying fest and never turned it back on. Since the rental car line seems to be in the middle of rush hour, I start checking my missed calls. The latest is from my parents, only twenty minutes ago. I'm sure they're worried like hell. It's been nine days since I last talked to them. I usually call on Sunday, when I can steal a few minutes from Mr. Ford's schedule.

I decide to surprise them instead and check the next missed call. I'm a little surprised it's Mr. Ford. I guess I threw his world in turmoil when I didn't show up today. Well, we're even on that score, at least. He'll have to put his big boy briefs on and wait for me to pick up where I left off in his office. Until I do, he'll be fine. Eventually, so will I… at least I think so. I erase his number from my contacts on a purely petty impulse. It's not like I won't recognize his number when he calls, again… and he will.

Suddenly, I'm standing at the checkout counter, where I convey my need for a car equipped for the weather. The clerk promises he can help me, then he takes my credit card and helps himself to the fee for the rental, before handing me a set of keys. After directing me to the rental car's parking lot on the north side of the building, I leave with my duffel bag on my shoulder, purse in my hand, looking for a red Jeep with all the amenities I need.

After a chilly walk in a light jacket, I find the vehicle. I toss my duffel bag in the back seat, my purse on the passenger's, and my ass in the driver's, then wait for the radiator to crank out heat through the vents. I start to sift through the missed text messages from the people that profess to love me. As expected, I encounter an angrily typed message from Mr. Ford.

720-596-0232: Where the hell are you, Malisa? I've been calling since Sunday night. I know you've checked out of the hotel today because I called. Get home immediately! We have work to do, and your parents are worried sick. At least call them back but get to work soon.

There's nothing to indicate that he still loves me or where we go from here. Well, actually, his text does tell me where we go from here.

Work.

I punch the trashcan icon at the top of my screen, deleting the text.

I read several messages from my parents, who are asking too many questions which I'll answer most of when I show up at their home unannounced. I ditch the phone in the passenger's seat and begin the drive to my childhood home. It's a modest two-story with nothing spectacular about it except the love that bursts out of every nook and cranny of it, and I need it.

The beauty of the scenery escapes me. Colorado is drop-dead gorgeous at this time of year. The sun reflects off the snow covering the ground in an impenetrable blanket of white. The Sangre de Cristo Mountains serve as a picturesque backdrop. If I sit here and wait, the base of the mountains will glow a reddish hue beneath the snow-covered peaks during setting of the sun. I get a little angry about not being happy to see any of it, after being away and too heartbroken to care.

A Couple of Forevers begins serenading me halfway through the fifteen-minute drive that I didn't even bother to turn the radio on for. Since the roads are treacherous at this time of year, even with the added terrain gear on the tires, I slow down to a crawl and reach for my cell. Jenna from Global Ford Enterprises is calling.

Things must really be bad at work if she's calling, I think. If I was feeling pettier, I wouldn't answer at all. Instead, I slam the phone to my ear and snap into the line, "Hello."

"Fuck, Malisa!" Mr. Ford snaps back. "Where the hell are you?"

The sound of his voice, even angry, is enough to break down the thin wall that took me two whole days to build to contain my turbulent emotions. I swallow convulsively, consuming the rising feelings before they get any farther up than my throat.

"Mr. Ford, what do you need?" My tone is much weaker than I would have preferred, but there's nothing I can do about it. Just struggling to keep my heartache back is taking more strength than I have.

"Mr. For…" he starts then pauses. He inhales loud enough for my receiver to pick up. "Malisa, I need you. Here. Now."

"I'll be back tomor…" My voice fades out entirely. I don't want to go back tomorrow or any other day if I didn't have him, but that isn't an option. *When* I go back is though.

"I'll be back tomorrow or next week. I'm not sure, but I'm positive that you can find someone to help you until then. Actually, you have someone already. Jenna! Make her do her damn job for once and consider this as me calling in and taking the vacation days I haven't used."

I hang up and drop the phone in my lap, before my mounting misery chokes the rest of my ability to speak out of me. The misery rebounds in my chest, apparently disliking being pushed down. I stop the truck on the side of the road, which has nonexistent traffic, mercifully. I only have to worry about killing just one person on the road while driving blinded by incoming tears.

I let the floodgates to my heartache open up.

It takes several minutes to get my emotions behind the thin wall patched up with lots of Band-Aids. I'm already tired of hurting and crying. I glimpse in the rearview mirror at my blotchy skin and swollen, red eyes. When I arrive at home, my parents are going to know something is up, if they don't already. Hopefully, I'll get to yell surprise before they start with the questions and I break down, again.

It's inevitable. I seem to be getting more miserable. My first real love has shattered my heart and the sound of his voice is working at the bits and pieces that is left of it. Still, I put the truck in drive and pull back onto the road, just before Chrisette sings out, again.

I cringe inside. Someone needs to teach Apollo when to stay, when to leave me alone, and when to quit calling, but the only someone available is me. I pick up the phone, and look down at the display screen, but it isn't Apollo calling or anyone else I know.

"Hello," I say into the earpiece, voice raspy and guttural from the number the tears just did on it.

"Malisa?" a familiar tone responds, but I can't place it.

"Who is this?"

"It's Derek." Then he laughs.

I think I missed the joke, and I probably would for a while.

"Are you okay, Malisa?"

"Ah… yes," I lie. "What can I do for you?"

He clears his throat. "Well, I was calling to see if you were available for meeting me tomorrow for a date, but you don't sound good. Can I do anything for you?"

Yep, mend my broken heart, I think to myself, willing to accept help from even the devil himself with no questions asked.

"Uh no, I'm in Colorado right now, Derek."

"No problem, I'm still in Vegas, only a flight away."

I don't have time for his agenda *and* my heartache.

"Derek, Colorado isn't exactly a dating state at this time of year, unless you have a ski suit to keep warm and boots to keep from landing on your backside. I won't be returning to Vegas, ever, or going back to Utah until tomorrow… or next week. I can't decide, so I think phone conversations are all I can give."

Anything else will just be too damn much.

"Want to tell me about it, Malisa?" His tone is sympathetic and undemanding, calling to every unshed tear that I have left.

"I'm… I can't, I'm…" I give up explaining and try to regroup, but the breaks in my voice are a dead giveaway for my emotional overload, which I don't think will ever let up.

I seem to just wear myself out, trying to get past it, and it just starts all over again with breaking me down. I'm supposed to be stronger than this.

"Dammit! I'm driving, Derek."

"And you're about to cry, so pull over. It's safer… *for everyone*," he adds dryly.

A trace of humor scales the heartache determined to break me, and it does what I can't; push the aching back so I can take his advice. I drive under the extended canopy of a local motel only five miles out from my parents.

"Okay, I'm off the road."

"What did your boss do, Malisa?"

Jesus! If Derek can figure out what went down, I have no hope of hiding it from my parents.

"How did you know?" I ask, so I can identify the signs that gave me away then hide them from everyone else.

"Malisa," he says dryly, "I'm a private eye. I notice a lot of things that other people don't. You and your boss have a very questionable tension between you two. I'd go so far as to say it's sexual. Now, what did he do between Saturday night and now that's driven you to Colorado instead of Utah?"

I'm busted, and don't have even a snowball's chance in hell of hiding sexual tension, but at least Apollo's attraction to me has already run its course.

I sigh, wishing it hadn't ended as soon as it began, and I'd rather keep the whole sordid and embarrassing one night of my relationship with my boss to myself. But my troubles are weighing heavily on my chest, and maybe telling someone about them will make the burden of carrying them a little easier. Since Derek and I don't run in the same circles and he's self-employed, I have no fear of becoming water cooler gossip. I begin to give him an earful of the best night and worst day of my life in between the constant beeps of someone calling my second line.

Chapter Nine

"Wow, Malisa, that has to be the fastest breakup not recorded."

I can't help laughing at his jab. "That's what I thought, too."

"Are you sure he's not just giving you space to cool down, though?"

My amusement flits away, allowing explosive anger to take its place.

"Who the hell needs two states of space? I only wanted him to calm down so I could explain that I was raised to do things for myself. So if a storm came, I wasn't blown over with my crutch. He blew out of the store like a Tasmanian devil and kept going before I could explain. But of course you'd take his side. It's the same crap your kind pulls and defends."

Derek's laughter rings outs. "My kind?"

"*Men!* The whole lot of you are *not* worth the trouble."

"And yet you're hurting over one of us?" he asks quietly.

I'm sure that question is rhetorical, so I say nothing.

"Listen, Malisa. I won't advise you to give him a second chance because I want my first chance with you. But I'm not sure if that's even possible, so I'll help you with your current love life anyway. I think you both overreacted. He didn't have to fly away at the first sign of trouble, especially since a man of his means should be thankful he wasn't dating a gold digger. But you're essentially quitting your job, breaching your contract. He could take you for everything you got."

"I know that, but he sent a message through a cab driver for me to stay away from work, for God's sake."

"Yeah, but as I said, I think he wanted you to calm down... or at least miss him. He obviously still cares or he'd have left you stranded altogether at that store. Now, he's calling for you to come home. Doesn't that tell you something?"

"Yes, it does. He needs a file," I spit.

Derek sniggers.

"Seriously, Malisa, you really think he could've built his company into the empire it is without being able to find a file? I can imagine him pulling chunks of his hair out though when he couldn't reach you for days, and I can promise you that he's regretting leaving in a hurry more than you regret getting involved with him."

"That's a *lot* of regret," I reply derisively.

"I saw the way he looked at you. He's suffering like hell. What are your plans for the time being? You won't stay down long if you're true to your upbringing, and you'll want to go back to work soon."

I haven't given that much thought to my future since it took a wrong turn on Sunday.

"I don't know anything, Derek, besides staying in Colorado for however long it takes me to stop crying."

"Laying low, nursing a broken heart until it's less damaged, huh? You know if you stay in one place long enough, he'll find you."

"Mr. Ford is too busy to look for me. Why would he when there are several gold diggers masquerading as ditzy socialites who won't think twice about spending his money, and they won't give him a hard time while doing it?"

"How many people do you know like Ford who chooses the easy way? He wouldn't be the man he is if he... Damn! Let me stop. I sound like I want to date him." Derek starts to laugh, and pulls a few more snickers out of me.

"Anyway, Derek, I'm just taking some time for myself, and I don't think you want to date someone laying low while nursing a broken heart caused by another man. But we can definitely be friends. God knows I need one of those."

He groans into the line, "Damn! I knew I'd been friend-zoned. I shouldn't have left you Saturday night."

I grunt. "Apollo had blocked any moves you were going to make just by being there."

"You love him, don't you?"

I nod, then realize that he can't see me. "I wish I didn't, but I do."

"Well, Malisa, I'll be glad to be your friend and take you out anyway. You need a shoulder to cry on, and I can't turn away a damsel in distress."

"Thanks, but you're a state over. I think letting me cry on your shoulder is well out of your way. And aren't you working?" That's at least one thing that I remember from our conversation Saturday night. Too bad my memory isn't spotty when it comes to Apollo.

"Yes, I'm on a job, but I have my own plane, a Cessna, so I'm mobile at all times as long as there's a runway. The person I'm surveilling will be here for another few days, so I could take you to breakfast and be back before my target gets up for lunch, which is usually when he wakes up after gambling away his wife's money and throwing it at strippers."

Derek's offer is sweet… and it could provide a distraction from me moping over Apollo every minute of the day and night.

"Alright, you convinced me. I'll pick you up at the airport around nine and take you to a little diner that I used to love while growing up here. Although, I'm not sure if it's still open. The owners were old when I was little."

He laughs, like I expected he would, his lightheartedness infectious and pushing away a little more of the gloom that's determined to surround me.

"But all I can promise you, Derek, is that we'll find something to eat, even if I have to cook it myself."

"Now, you're talking, Malisa. I can't remember the last home cooked anything I had. I'm gone from home so much I think I have airplane ass."

"What does airplane ass look like, Derek?" I ask, between peals of laughter.

He stops chuckling, suddenly, like he's seriously considering the question.

"I don't know to tell you the truth." He really was considering it, which just makes me laugh even harder.

A pecking on the window behind me traps my laughter in my throat. Completely startled, I jerk my head around in the direction of the knock. A white man stands at the rear of the Jeep, with his hand perched on top of something strapped to his hip and a brown Stetson hat on his head. The sunlight reflects a badge pinned to the center of his hat. Then I notice his brown uniform and patrol car parked behind mine.

I squeal, "Oh God, it's the cops!"

"What's happening, Malisa?" Derek asks, worriedly.

"Hold on, and I'll find out," I say hurriedly, then roll down my window. "Yes, officer?"

"Ma'am, the owner of this motel that you're parked in front of isn't sure if you're planning to rob the place or not."

"What? No!" I jerk the phone from my ear and extend it out the window. "I just pulled over to take a call. I didn't want to be a hazard on the road." For various reasons, most of which I intend to keep to myself.

"That's fine, but you're going to have to pull over somewhere else. Mr. Lindsey is old and easily spooked," the sheriff says, dryly.

I guess he's taken several phone calls from a spooked Mr. Lindsey.

"Okay, officer, thank you," I respond quickly—happy that I won't be spending a night in jail under suspicion of attempted robbery.

Then I slam the phone back to my ear.

"Derek, I have to go. Call me when you arrive in the morning."

I look in the side mirror at the cop who's still watching me, while I put the truck in gear.

"Okay, Malisa, but text me and let me know you got to your parents' safely or I'll be worried about you, like everyone else seems to be."

"Okay. Bye, Derek."

I toss the phone in the passenger seat and drive away slowly, then speed up when I've left the cop in the distance. He appears in my rearview mirror seconds later, half a mile away. Now, I'm the one that's spooked. Maybe he still thinks I'm a lone cat burglar targeting motels with aging owners in the snow-covered countryside.

Man, loving Apollo has taken me to some low places, I think and laugh nervously.

The last few minutes of my trip to home are uneventful, thankfully. When I finally arrive, the long driveway is filled with cars up to the side of the house. My first instinct is to believe that my parents are having a party. I hope they have enough room and food for one gate-crashing daughter who's parking behind the last car in the driveway, leaving room for only one more. The rest of the guests arriving late are stuck with parking beside the road in the frozen drainage ditch.

I send Derek a quit text that I've made it home, then toss the phone in my purse, to collect with my other things. I get out of the Jeep, stuffing the keys in my jacket's pocket, just as the cop's car drives into the driveway then parks behind me.

Holy hell!

I stand, as frozen as the drainage ditch, beside the rental truck. The sheriff gets out of his cruiser and shoves the Stetson on his head. I wait, horrified that he's coming to arrest me anyway, except I haven't done anything wrong.

He starts walking in my direction.

"Ma'am, do you know these people?" he asks, with a very distrustful expression on his face.

I start to wonder if this is a prime example of racial profiling. Why can't a black girl have parents who've owned a two-story, brown-bricked home for the last twenty-six years?

Since I want to know who I was going to file a discrimination report on in the local sheriff's office in the morning, I start to scrutinize the officer. I've already mentally filed away the short, blond buzz cut and medium-sized ears that I managed to see before he put his hat on.

As he gets closer, the rest of his features come into view; piercing blue eyes, a chiseled jaw line with cleft chin, straight nose on top of lush, pink lips, hulking shoulders over long legs that fill out his uniform nicely and puts him in the above average height category.

Something begins to nag at my conscience about his face. I swear I used to see a softer version of it five times a week at school and just about every weekend, whenever my parents babysat Blake for his parents. They were frequently jet-setting to one warm place or another without their son.

"*Blake*," I shriek, thoroughly shocked that he's anywhere near Arrow.

He promised to ship out with the Army and never return, after a heated argument with his parents. Yet, he's here, stopping in his tracks, and frowning at me.

"Malisa?" he whispers, just as shook as I am.

I nod. He walks closer to stare down into my face like I'm some damn lab specimen. I stomp my foot, when it seems like he's never going to accept that it's really me. Maybe the makeover was a bad idea, after all.

"Blake, it's me!"

His face splits wide with a grin. "Yeah, it's you who still gets pissy quick."

Then he opens his arms wide and lunges for me. I lunge toward him, more than ready to exchange my sisterly hug for his brotherly one, which we often gave each other whenever his parents dumped him like a load of dirty laundry on my parents' doorstep.

His arms tighten around me. "I missed you, big city girl."

"I missed you too, Blake, though I assumed you'd still be off somewhere other than here."

He releases me and steps back, before I'm ready. Being in his arms or my parents' is the same as being home. I wanted to be home so badly, to find the glue that would mend the broken pieces of my heart back together. Besides Apollo, my family are the only ones with that power.

Blake straightens the brown jacket that matches the slacks of his uniform.

"I was stationed in Japan, until my father had a stroke two years ago. I almost didn't come back, but they begged me to." He shrugs. "So here I am. A military cop in a small-town sheriff's position, responding to nuisance callers and sometimes finding lost women by accident."

I cock an eyebrow in confusion.

"Sorry about your father, and who was lost?"

"*You* were, Malisa. I came to file a missing person's report for Lydia and Frank Owens. Your boyfriend called here Sunday night to see if you were here, after going on vacation. When Lydia and Frank had to say no, they got worried. I had to wait twenty-four hours before I could officially file a missing person's report. When you didn't turn up last night, I came to do the paperwork this morning, but you were always good at taking care of yourself."

Oh damn! My parents called the cops, and the cop that showed up is Blake!

I twist at the waist, taking in all the cars littering the yard that probably belong to the rest of the family.

"I don't have a boyfriend, and this is a damn search party," I mumble, as I swivel back around to Blake.

If my missing-in-action status has gotten around this fast, I can only imagine how fast the troubles in my personal life will spread.

"Yes, Malisa, this is a damn search party and it's good to know that you're still intelligent. Now that you're here, I can get reacquainted with my sister who disappeared then showed up out of thin air looking like a model. Your boss has been calling here like an overeager bloodhound who said he was your boyfriend, by the way. Any cop with his salt can tell he had some guilt in you going AWOL." Blake's eyes roam over me. "What in the hell have you done to yourself, Malisa?"

Yep, Blake is still the same brother that I never had, teasing me about everything right and wrong with me. A silly grin spreads across my face. I'm sort of glad that the stupid antics of his didn't disappear with time, and I'm sort of not glad.

"I had a makeover, Blake." And it cost me someone dear in the process who's still claiming to be my man.

He shifts his weight to one foot and begins to rub his clean-shaven jaw absentmindedly, while propping a hand on his supporting hip.

"Well, I liked the glasses and pigtails better, but if this is what you prefer…" He waves a hand in front of me, dismissively. "…fine by—"

"*You found her, Blake!*" my mother screams from behind me.

I turn around just in time to see her descend the three steps of her raised front porch, at a breakneck pace. She has more gray sprinkled through the edges of her shoulder-length hair than I remember. It's flying out around the carbon copy of my face, except my mother has always been pretty. Her features never seemed to look right on me, and I often called myself her ugly duckling. She hated that and often told me off about cutting myself down.

I didn't stop doing it, until she threatened to spank me at the ripe old age of thirteen. She always promised I'd grow into a beautiful woman one day. Well, I don't know if that will ever happen, but I'm definitely not her ugly duckling anymore.

I prepare for her embrace, by opening my arms wide. She crashes into me, and nearly takes us both down to the ground.

"My baby has come home! I've been so worried about you," she says, before stepping back to run her hands down my arms. She's smiling hard enough to crack her face, or at least add one more laugh wrinkle around her mouth. "Now, where have you been? And what did you do to yourself? My baby girl is gone. And why are you sad?"

"Surprise," I say dryly instead, still not ready to tell all. At least not in front of Blake, who'll just crack a joke at my broken heart's expense.

Chapter Ten

Lydia purses her lips. "Surprise yourself, Malisa. Now answer my questions."

I point toward the front door of the house. "Can I go inside first? It's cold out here."

The light jacket lets the wind frisk my body every time the hugs stop. Lydia's mouth twists to the side. She plants her hands on her curvy hips draped in designer jeans enclosed in flat, black riding boots, as if she has to think about letting her only daughter through the front door of her home.

"Mama!" I shriek.

"She's pissy again," Blake grumbles, good-naturedly, from behind me.

Lydia starts to giggle. "I don't have to tell you to go in your own house, sweetheart. Tell your father hello before he chokes his brother, Tommy, who's teasing Frank about you being abducted into a white slavery ring. It doesn't matter how much Tommy emphasizes *white* slavery, it just passes right over Frank's head. Blake and I will bring in your bags to your old room."

I'd stirred up a real hornet's nest with just switching off my cell phone for a few days, and now the whole damn family is here. My father has two brothers and three sisters, most with kids of every age of their own. My mother, like me, is an only child. Like most kids with no siblings, Lydia wanted more children to raise on my father's pediatrician income, but it wasn't meant to be.

Hence Blake being loved like he was born from my parents, and it doesn't matter to them that he's white. We were both taught to judge people for their actions, not their skin color, and we were both subjected to Lydia's rare spankings and regular punishments when we did something wrong.

I walk toward the house, which still looks the same after being renovated inside and out just before I left for college. I enter the front door quietly, laughter and chatter escaping from the den's doorway just off the left of the great room that I'm walking through. The den should've been a guest bedroom, but with four bedrooms upstairs at the top of the staircase that's climbing up the wall on my right, my father got a man cave instead.

The wide doorway in front of me opens into a long, narrow kitchen, which was the most cheerful place in this house when I lived here. On each side of the double farm sinks are two bay windows that let sunlight pour in, nourishing my mother's plants spread throughout most of the first level. They're just as old as me and Blake. Their vines grow haphazardly from tables positioned behind the couch and against the walls.

If everyone that visits here knows what's good for them, they'll treat those plants like human beings and avoid them like the plague. Mama treats them like they're her children, and we do well when we respect that. I take a deep breath and stand still in the middle of the deep burgundy, Victorian furniture that is for show, but not for sitting. I absorb the love that's flooding the house right along with the sunlight.

"Daddy!" I yell. All the noise in the den ceases.

"Malisa!" he yells back.

Uncle Tommy steps into the opened doorway of the den first, laughs, and then looks back over his shoulder. "How many other people call you daddy, Frank... besides Lydia," he quips, then turns to stare at me.

I just smile back. Tommy Owens will never change, a wannabe comedian with no filter that's hilarious to everyone but my father, who walks up behind Tommy finally. Frank's wide shoulders droop in relief when he sees me.

"My baby girl," he whispers.

For a moment, daddy and I only see each other. Neither of us could ever do anything wrong in the other's eyes. This drove my mother crazy, especially when he wouldn't help her discipline me as a child.

"That's not my little niece anymore, Frank," Tommy says suddenly, breaking the spell. "That's a woman."

Frank's head swings to the side to glare down at Tommy, who's a head shorter and a whole house lighter than my father.

"Shut up, Tommy." My father gives his usual response to anything his brother says, which is usually a joke at my father's expense.

It's not uncommon for all my father's siblings to have already worked his nerves in the first few minutes of their visits, but he'd kill for all of us.

Frank elbows his way past Tommy, who chuckles wildly, as he collides with the wall outside the den. Daddy's arms embrace me in a bear hug that often swallows up the receiver. My father's bulky frame is intimidating until you discover the gentle giant beneath his chocolate skin. He lets Blake and I get away with murder countless times, until my mother found out about whatever we'd done, then there was hell to pay. Usually, Frank went down in flames right along with us. But he's the only one who can swing her moods back to peaceful.

"I'm glad you're home, baby girl." His voice is gruff against my ear.

I can imagine his thick lips stretching across this face as he smiles beneath the large nose that fits his face perfectly.

"Me too, daddy. I missed you," I say into his wide chest, covered in a plaid, button down shirt over jeans.

Just as the front opens behind me and gives me a chill, my father steps back and pens me with a worried glance from wide set, jet black eyes.

"Where in the hell have you been, baby girl?"

"Daddy, I'm fine. I was at a hotel on vacation in Vegas. I left this morning, after taking a couple of more days for myself. I really needed it."

Frank frowns. "Your boss works you *that* hard?"

"He did, but I fixed it. That's why I'm here."

I know I'm making light of the situation that has caused me so much pain, but the different versions of older Owens in their late thirties and early forties have walked into the great room. M y aunts, Chrysalis, and twins, Barbie and Jen, along with my other uncle Luke, the baby of the older Owens clan are all listening. That's too many ears for my liking.

"So, you're here to stay?" Blake asks, from behind me.

I turn around, with my hands still resting on my father's shoulders. Blake, with my duffel bag in his hand, stops at the bottom of the stairs. My mother, with my purse and cell phone in hers, are walking up them.

"No, but I'm here for at least a couple days."

That brings a grin to Blake's face, which probably doesn't mean anything good for me.

"Good, Malisa. Picking on people is frowned upon when you're a cop, but *you* are my sister, so that makes it okay."

"Mom!" I yell, just like old times, hoping to warn Blake off from the practical jokes and teasing that he'll do, with no everlasting damage.

It's still annoying, though.

Everyone laughs at my distress. I don't want to imagine what they'll do if they find out about Apollo. Lydia pauses midway up the steps then looks down at her hand, just before my cell phone rings in it.

"Don't answer it!" I shout, but my mother's already swiping the accept icon and raising the phone to her ear.

She shrugs and says sweetly into the mouthpiece, "Hello."

I hang my head, and sigh. Nothing's changed with her, either. She still does what she wants to, and that could be because she's the product of a mob boss, or so my father claimed almost daily when I lived here.

Uncle Tommy sets loose a round of his hefty laughter, for such a short man.

"Must be the stalker," he quips.

He's no better than Blake.

"What stalker?" Blake demands, in a steely voice that he uses when *he's* pissy, and no good will come of it.

Shit! Shit! Shit!

My head snaps up. "I don't have a stalker, Blake."

"Bull swanky, kid," Tommy pipes in. "Your boss has been calling here every few hours since Sunday, checking to see if you've snuck out of the hotel and showed up here in the spur of the moment road trip. Looks like he was onto something, when he couldn't get you on the horn and no one else had seen hide nor hair of you. As soon as Lydia tells him that you're here, she'll have another guest to put up… with," he adds in a nonchalant tone, as if my boss showing up here would be normal.

But Uncle Tommy may be onto something. Yet, I can't be sure if he is or isn't, while standing down here with him. I turn, to run for the stairs, just as my mother okay's something.

No no no!

"Mama, give me the phone please!"

She laughs into the receiver instead. "Yes, Mr. Ford, our house is fifteen miles from the airport on a straightaway. You can't miss—"

"No mama!" I yell, waving my hands like I'm directing a fleet of aircraft, while taking the steps two at a time.

She cuts her eyes my way then turns her back, and finishes climbing the stairs. "Okay… Apollo, it is… No, you want be imposing. We'll be glad to have you."

Holy, holy hell!

I reach her just as she tops the staircase. Then I reach around her to snatch the phone from her hand, and run back down the steps and out the front door as if my life depends on it. Well, my broken heart depends on it anyway. I stop beside the Jeep.

"Mr. Ford, don't come here," I gasp, breathless from the only workout I've intentionally took part in, in my entire life.

He says nothing.

"Mr. Ford—"

"I'm still here, Malisa… and I'm still coming. I need to talk to you, face to face."

I bend over, trying to place my head between my knees. I don't know if the running has made me lightheaded, or it's simply because I ceased to breathe when Apollo said he needed to talk to me, face to face. Both are probably a contributing factor.

"No… you don't get… to do that," I pant.

"Malisa, I know I shouldn't have left Vegas, but I was angry… and hurt. Sweetheart—"

"Don't!" I cut him off, before he wakes the sleeping storm of my emotions. I wasn't going to give him any more opportunities to pull my heart even more to his side. "You weren't the only one hurt. Let me go. Well, actually… Jesus, where's the air… I should say stay away, since you've already let me go, but I'll be back at work in at least a few days, so don't call your lawyers."

"I can't let you go, my Lisa," he whispers.

A bolt of lightning streaks through my abdomen and upward into my chest. My heart absorbs the electrical current, which sends my heartrate through the roof. Now, I really can't breathe. When will I stop being affected by Apollo?

I don't know if that is even a possibility, which makes me angry.

"You did let me go, Apollo. Now leave it that way. If you wait a few weeks, you'll forget about what happened the other night and the day after. It was that short of a relationship."

"Have you forgotten?" he asks softly, just as someone walks up behind me.

"Malisa," Blake yells, making me spin around.

Privacy is a pipe dream at 256 Dillard Lane.

"Who is that?" Apollo asks, the whisper of his voice now a cold, steely, and demanding murmur.

"The cops!" I snap. "So, stay away, Mr. Ford."

Blake reaches out an empty hand to me. "Give me the phone, Lisa Poo."

I cringe, hating that nickname, which has a disgusting origin thanks to Blake, and yes it involves poo of course.

"No, Blake. I got this." Then I shake my head and begin to back away.

Apollo hisses in my ear. "Malisa!"

"Mr. Ford, please don't come here." I beg, while stepping back from an advancing Blake, who's still reaching for the phone.

"Malisa, you owe me the chance to explain."

Owe him? I'd already given him everything, and he still wants *more*?

I grow rigid with fury and forget to keep stepping away from Blake. "You have a lot of nerve, Apollo, to think—" Blake lunges forward and rips the phone from my ear before I can finish. I don't miss the irony of doing that to Lydia, and now Blake has done it to me.

I'll apologize to my mother later. Right now, I need my phone back, which is going to be next to impossible. I grow more and more horrified as Blake puts the phone to his ear, while wearing one of his mischievous smiles, which is the reason for my horror. The next few minutes aren't going to play out well for me, either, and this is how they'll go...

I'll start to jump, reaching for whatever Blake has snatched from me, hoping to rise above his towering frame and take it back. He's about six four now at twenty-six years old, but I won't get any taller than five four, at twenty-five. This is where the 'next to impossible' comes in. I won't get back what Blake has taken from me until he's ready for me to have it. Yet, I'll try desperately to get it anyway, before he decides to give it back.

Like I said, nothing's changed at my childhood home. Blake's still the harmless bully, I his helpless victim, who grabs a fistful of his sheriff's jacket and starts to jump and grab for the phone pressed to his ear, and miss.

I scream, "Give. Me. The. Damn. Phone."

Blake keeps the phone. "Hello."

I resort to calling for backup, while leap frogging and coming up empty-handed, "Mama."

Blake just moves in time with my pointless jumps, twisting his head out of the way of my desperate grabs, and I come away empty-handed, pitifully.

"This is Sheriff Powers with Arrow's Sheriff Department. Who am I speaking with?" he asks in an official, authoritative tone, which I've never heard him use before.

It's probably reserved for those he's about to arrest. That won't stop me from assaulting him if it gets my phone back though.

"Dammit all to hell! Give me the phone, Blake! Mama!"

He tilts his head to the side. "Oh, *you're* the Apollo Ford that's kept my sister away from home. Care to tell me why she decided to disappear then just show up at home when we haven't seen her in all this time?"

More panic overwhelms me, and I stop jumping so the escalating feeling can take me over in peace.

"That's not your business, Blake," I growl low, hoping Apollo will keep quiet like he did when he chose to just fly out of my life.

But just in case he decides to unburden himself, I start to scream my mother's name repeatedly so Blake can't hear, and make more desperate jumps for the phone, again. He spins away. I follow the side of him that has the phone, which puts my back to the front door of the house. When he grins down at me, I wonder where the hell my mother is. Lydia should've been out here ages ago.

"Mr. Ford... Well, sure I'll call you Apollo, and you're welcome to come down. We'd love to have you for a few days... Yep, I'll meet you in the morning about nine. Bye now." Then Blake presses the phone into my chest gently.

I clasp my hand around the phone, holding it tightly to my chest, which is filling up with pure dread. Apollo isn't the only one coming here in the morning.

"Dammit, Blake, do you know what you've done?" I ask, barely above a whisper, anxiety compressing my lungs.

He shrugs. "I offered to meet your boss and show him how to get here then find out what happened between you two."

"It's none of your business what he's done, and I'm already meeting someone else at the airport in the morning!" Suddenly, I regret coming home, and step back from Blake. "I shouldn't have come here."

I hadn't come home to unburden the woes of my limited love life on my family, just absorb their love so it would repair the damage Apollo had done. But my road trip backfired. Two totally different men will show up at my parents' home in the morning, and it's just a matter of time before my love for my boss becomes everyone's business.

But not if I leave first.

93

Chapter Eleven

Blake pulls his own cell phone from his pocket. I start to realize just how much of an insensitive cad he is. I walk away, leaving him standing on the driveway alone. I have to pass by the whole Owens clan, my parents included. They've miraculously appeared on the front porch after Blake mucked up the rest of my life. If everyone is waiting for more drama to erupt at my expense, they all better buy a crystal ball, because I'm putting as much distance as I can between me and Arrow.

Inside the house, I take the stairs two at time. At top of the staircase, I pass by one long hallway on my immediate left that leads into my parents' room and overlooks the second level, to walk straight into the hallway for the other three, much smaller bedrooms. The guest bedroom sits alone on the left side of the hallway, often unused. On the opposite side are the two bedrooms filled with mine and Blake's childhoods.

My old room is at the end of the second level. The squeaky floorboards between my bedroom and Blake's still give me away. It's weird that the floor still squeaks under the plush, gray carpet, even after the renovation. When I'm inside my room, I lock the door behind me, and my childhood space is still decorated in pale pink, sky blue, and pine wood furniture. The room seems so tiny now, the en suite bathroom even tinier, when compared to the master bedroom in my apartment and the one I spent Saturday night in with Apollo.

Don't think about that, Malisa, at least not right now.

I begin to make plans for my return trip to Utah, much sooner than I'd like to go, but I can't stay at my parents' home. There's no peaceful way to grieve Apollo here, not with everyone up in my business. I guess it's true that you can't go home again.

I sit down on the striped comforter on my twin bed, beside my duffel bed and purse, which holds my plane ticket with the airport's number on it. After punching the numbers in my phone, I wait for someone to pick up. Just as the ringing line is replaced with a greeting from a live operator, someone knocks at my bedroom door.

I ignore the knock and request a flight out as soon as possible.

"Your name, ma'am?" The operator's voice sounds identical to the one that companies, from small to Fortune 500, seem to use for their automated systems, making me think that this lady has been doing this job for too damn long.

"My name is Malisa Owens."

A knock trespasses against the door again, and then the knob turns wildly.

"Malisa!" Blake yells through the wooden barrier, then bangs on the door.

I ignore that, too.

"Ma'am, is your address 137 Woodard Lane Apt B in Lake City, Utah?"

"Yes," I answer, warily. "Why does that matter?"

"Because you're on the no-fly list," she responds dryly.

No fly?

"What? I just flew in!"

Blake stops banging and yelling through the door.

"Yes, you just arrived in Colorado only a couple of hours ago, but you've just been added to the no-fly list only minutes ago, by... Sheriff Blake Powers of Arrow, Colorado."

"*Are you fucking kidding me?*" I scream, but I didn't mean to do it in the operator's ear... no, that's a lie. I am fucking furious. Blake has literally grounded me.

"No Ms. Owens, I'm not kidding. Goodbye." The operator even manages to say that robotically, before promptly hanging the hell up on me.

All I can do is stare at the phone in disbelief.

Blake starts turning the knob wildly, again, drawing my attention from my cell phone.

"Malisa, open the door, please."

"Blake!" I yell, almost hysterical, "I think you've done enough damage for one day! Go away!"

I lean over to stuff the useless ticket back in my purse violently. I rattle the Jeep's keys in my pocket. I grin, and the heightened state of my emotions settle. Maybe I can't fly out of Colorado, but I sure as hell can drive away from Arrow. Eventually, Blake has to go to work, and everyone else has to go to sleep, if they all don't just go home first.

I hear a thump against the door, followed by Blake saying, "I didn't mean to piss you off, Lisa Poo." His voice is muffled.

"Seriously, Blake," I snap, and my emotions, which I'm beginning to refer to as whirlwind, kick back into high gear. "You put me on the no-fly list like I'm a goddamn domestic terrorist, and you thought you wouldn't piss me the hell *off*? I would never do something like that to you. You are officially just a cop to me. Now go harass someone else."

"Malisa, I don't want you running off. I can just as easily call and have you taken you off the list."

"Talk to me when you have!"

"Not until you tell me why you cut everyone off and then showed up at home, after four years."

"I only owe my family that explanation, and they haven't asked." Everyone had only wanted to know where the hell had I been—a much easier question to answer.

"You'll always be my family, Lisa Poo. Without the Owens, I don't know where I'd be."

He had a funny way of showing his appreciation.

Another thump echoes through the door. "I know something's wrong, Malisa, and you're running from it… or your boss. But you have to let me in so I can fix it, little sister."

I have nothing to say. It seems no one can fix my heartbreak but Apollo. But I'm terrified of getting back with him, which means I'm stuck with waiting for time to dull the pain and for Blake to take me off the no-fly list.

"I'm sorry, Malisa. I didn't mean to hurt you.".

"Blake, you're a damn bully! Of course, you mean to hurt me." But he's never gone this far before.

"It was always in fun, little sister, and I'm worried about you. Everyone is. You need to stay put so we can work through whatever's bothering you. That's all we want."

His tone may be filled with regret, but I don't care. I'd suffered enough for the last three days, and he's blocked the only way I have of coping with my heartbreak—leaving to find a place where I can heal. As long as my air travels are blocked and I'm essentially stuck in Colorado, I have nothing to say to him or anyone else.

"Go away, Blake."

"Jeez, Malisa, just open the door," he whines, in a deep tenor not meant for whining.

"I don't think so, Blake. You'll probably take my phone and invite someone else here that I don't want to see right now."

"Again, I'm sorry, Lisa Poo, and I'll fix it… somehow. But what did your boss do to you?"

"Again, I don't want to talk about it."

I burrow my head under the mountain of pink and blue pillows at the head of my bed, muffling any sound that may come through the door next. Suddenly, I feel as if I can't keep my eyes open. Maintaining a broken heart and an angry dialogue is exhausting. I decide to catch a nap, at least for a couple of hours, then call Derek to cancel breakfast on my way away from here. I couldn't find the street in this condition, but this house isn't home anymore. Not when the man that hurt me is welcome to visit.

It's a mistake to intentionally remember Apollo, as if I could forget him. The stupid tears make an appearance. I let them roll where they may, mainly soaking the mattress until sleep comes for me, along with the nightmare of Apollo showing up to meet my parents, with one of the ditzy socialites he'd dated in Utah. I jerk to consciousness and snap my eyes open, while laying on my side.

Once the contacts adjust on my eyeballs, I get an up close and too damn personal view of the wall that I'm also pressed into face first, by a body that's pressing into mine from behind. Warm breath fans the back of my neck. It's impossible to turn over, to see who had broken into my room during the night and climbed into bed with me, though the room is full of morning light.

Shit! How did I sleep for the rest of the day and night instead of a couple of hours? And Derek is probably already on his way here. Why didn't I cancel breakfast with him before I went to damn sleep? One more stupid move for the books, Malisa.

However, I have an idea of who committed the stupid move of violating my bedroom. I glimpse over my shoulder and get a side shot of the tip of Blake's shoulders in his wrinkled sheriff's uniform, just as my mother's voice rings out in the hallway, on the other side of the closed door.

"Blake," I call grumpily.

"Dammit, Lisa Poo," he responds before rolling over then settles right back into a sound sleep, like I expected him to.

Finding him in my bed or on a thick pallet beside it isn't unusual. I should've known that he'd get in this room one way or the another. As a child, he was always in here, instead of in his, which is one room up from mine. But we're not children, or even teenagers for that matter, and I'm still pissy about what he did to me yesterday. Yet, it's almost impossible to wake him in the morning, or stay completely angry with him.

I climb out of the wall to a sitting position and push my hair out of my face in time to see the doorknob turn. I sit and wait for my mother to walk in, so she can find Blake in my bed, then get him out of it. She's one of the only two people who can.

The door opens, finally. Lydia materializes in the doorway with Derek and Apollo standing behind her with different emotions ranging in their faces. My mother appears smug, Derek amused, and Apollo, well, he just seems pissy.

I gasp, surprised. My stomach drops into my abdomen. My heart stalls out. Then I panic, shut my eyes, and begin to pray that I just saw people who aren't really there, even while the image of Apollo is crystallizing on my brain. If I wanted another shot of getting back with him, well, that's been shot all to hell now, and he's still too damn beautiful to look at.

"Malisa and Blake," my mother calls sweetly. "It's eight o'clock and time to get up."

If she's really here, so is Derek and Apollo. Together. And both are too damn early.

Oh my damn! I should've left last night.

But it's too late for that, so I open my eyes. Suddenly, the room is much bigger, or maybe it's just my eyes that are bigger.

Why do I feel like I've been caught cheating?

"Hey… everyone," I mutter under my breath, brave enough to make eye contact with only my mother.

Blake sits up beside me, looks at everyone standing in the doorway, and grins. I can only imagine what Derek and Apollo are thinking. At least I'm fully clothed, and that's my only consolation on this day that is starting out just plain wrong.

Derek covers his mouth with one hand, but it doesn't contain his quiet laughter. "You're adorable when you wake up, Malisa."

I cringe inwardly. "I'm sure you're the only one that thinks so, Derek. By the way, why is everyone standing outside my room?"

Apollo shifts his weight, drawing my attention. He steps around my mother, and then inside the room.

"Is that better?" he asks sarcastically. His eyes cut me wide open.

I know that look well. I've touched a nerve, and that's never a good thing to do with Apollo. I seem to be doing all the wrong things concerning him lately, and it started the minute I allowed him to become more than my boss.

I swallow hard, before answering, "Actually, it's not better, Mr. Ford. How did you get here?"

"I drove," he deadpans. "With Derek calling shotgun. I didn't want to bother Sheriff Powers at the station or your family when I had a perfectly good GPS system in my rental. And Derek was at the airport waiting for you to pick him up. I couldn't exactly leave him standing beside his plane on the tarmac, now could I?"

Apollo's explanation takes me by surprise. He has to be absolutely secure within himself to give a ride to a man that wants to date the same woman as he does. It's going to be interesting when he realizes that Blake and Sheriff Powers are one and the same, and in the bed beside me. However, I'm more interested in the part where Apollo said he drove here. I've never seen him take time to drive a ball down the golf course, even less a car. And since when does he wear casual white, Polo shirts and dark blue jeans with designer bleach spots on the thighs, with white hiking boots?

They fit him just as beautifully as his suits do.

"I didn't know you could drive, Mr. Ford."

"Doesn't mean I can't do it. It's hard to do when you and I are going over details for my next piece of business, isn't it? That's why I have a full-time driver."

That makes sense.

"Well, you probably need to make finding my replacement your next piece of business, because I need you to let me out of my contract early, please."

My heart still can't imagine working with him without being with him, even when my mind knows that's probably the best thing for everyone involved, especially my heart. Whether it wants to accept it or not.

"Not a chance, Malisa," he spits from low in his throat. "The contract between us is there for a reason, so my assistant for the next nine months is right here... sleeping with another man."

I suspect he's gritting his teeth, too, still angry as hell with me... and possibly jealous. This just makes me angry. He doesn't have the right to be anything, when he pushed me a whole state away.

"Be glad that's all we were doing, Mr. Ford. You should enjoy the next nine months, because I'm done being absorbed into your life and missing out on mine. And for the record, the other man is my emotionally-demanding, adopted brother, Blake. Blake meet Apollo and the grinning jack behind mama, Derek."

Blake sniggers. "I'm a cop, Lisa Poo. I got all that already. Now what's for breakfast?"

My mother and two men just walked in on us in the same bed together, albeit fully-clothed, and he wants breakfast, when the new reason for Apollo being angry with me is all his fault. I reach behind me, grab a pillow, and swing it at Blake's head, which he easily blocks with his forearm and gets to his feet.

"Seriously, do you ever do anything besides harass me, muck my life up, and eat, Blake?"

He's still a walking parasite on two legs that consumes everything edible.

"Nope," he responds casually, and then tucks the stray tails of his shirt into his slacks, making the situation even more awkward, at least for me. "Harassing you, Lisa Poo, mucking up your life, and eating are the most important things in this world to me. But not necessarily in that order. Mama O, I'm hungry, and Lisa Poo just assaulted a cop. Spank her. Where's Pop?"

Lydia points behind her with a thumb thrown over her shoulder. "In his den with the other family, and breakfast will be cooked by Malisa. I'm taking a break today."

I scoff, "In other words, you're going to be all up in my business."

She grins. "Yep, so get up, baby girl. Shower, dress, and please comb your hair. It's everywhere. Apollo and Derek, follow me."

She turns on her heels and walks away. Derek and Blake trail her out of the room. Apollo stands his ground, while eyeballing me while I undoubtedly look a mess. I raise my hands to my head, to cover up at least the sides of my bedhead. His intense stare makes heat spike in my blood, which is already rushing through my veins and creating its own warmth. I'm destined to always be too hot around this man, and I should just get used to it.

"You're beautiful, my Lisa," he whispers, and adds a little more heat to my system. He is sure to put emphasis on the word *my*.

"That's not…" I pause, thinking it would be rather rude and ungrateful to throw his compliment back at him. That's how we got in this mess in the first place.

I exhale, wishing for a cool breeze, and let my hands drop to my knees. He's already seen the bird's nest on my head, but I'm wondering why is he still here, in my bedroom.

"Thank you, Mr. Ford. Now what can I do for you?"

He wastes no time replying, "Talk to me."

I know that's exactly what we need to do, even if he just needs to smooth things over with his best employee. I won't be after my contract is up.

There's nowhere to have a private conversation at my parents' house about anything.

"I would talk to you, if we were somewhere else. Privacy is but a dream around here. My mother *will* be back at any second, to interrupt. She doesn't like when her commands are ignored."

Lydia materializes in my doorway, as if I've summoned her with magic. "You're right, baby girl, and I'm already back, interrupting."

Apollo glances back at my mother, before retraining his eyes on me, again. "Just promise me that'll you hear me out before we leave for Utah."

I can certainly hear him out, but leaving today isn't going to work for me.

"Mr. Ford, I need to use some of my vacation time to just take some time for myself. At least a week... or two."

His shifts his weight to one foot and drops his suddenly tightly-clenched fists to his side. "I can't agree to that, Malisa. If you want me to hire another PA, you'll have to start training her right away. You practically run my company singlehandedly, and it'll take the next nine months, if not longer, to find someone who is as capable as you are in the office. You can take your vacation time off the back end of your contract. You have two months' worth."

I find it hard to believe that he's willing to reduce my sentence by two months and taking my advice about hiring a second PA, finally, but at least something's changed between us. Even the catch-22 that I've lived in on the edge of his world has morphed in conditions; I'm not secretly loving him anymore. He knows it now. It didn't work out, and yet I still have to work with him. I'm still damned if do, damned if I don't, and it's true that the more things change, the more they stay the same. I no longer see the point in trying to fight the system that Apollo's put in place around me. It doesn't seem to do me any good.

"Fine, I'll fly out tonight... if I can, and be at work bright and early tomorrow, to put the word out that you'll looking for a new PA."

I agree to this, because I have the feeling that my heart won't heal until I do.

"Thank you, Malisa. See you downstairs." Apollo takes a step toward me then stops, and just stares. His eyes darken. His gaze intensifies until a ball of pressure emerges in my core then discharges as ripples that encompass my whole body and impact my lungs. I visibly tremble from the force of the alien energy moving through me, and then it settles between my thighs as a steady throb.

What the fuck was that?

My chest heaves, as I suck up all the air to replace what suddenly went missing from my lungs. Apollo smiles with just one side of his mouth then turns away, but the magical exhibition he performed with just a look sticks with me.

Chapter Twelve

My mother and I watch him walk toward her, pass by her in the doorway, and then vanish in the hallway. When I think he has arrived at the bottom of the stairs, Lydia takes a seat on the bed.

"Mama, why did you bring them up here?" I ask, while still reeling from the effects of Apollo's visual attack on my body. "You had to know Blake was in the bed with me."

Not much gets by her in her house, and she'd stuck me in the most uncomfortable of positions. She and Blake don't seem to care what everyone else will think when they find out what just happened, but I sure as hell do.

She smirks. "I knew exactly where Blake was. Apollo needs to be taught a few lessons, like other men will quickly fill his shoes if he doesn't stick around to wear them himself."

I close my eyes and grumble, "Is there such a thing as privacy around here anywhere? You heard for yourself, mama, that we are *not* getting back together."

Sympathy rolls through her face like an incoming hurricane taking over a city. "How do you feel about that, baby girl?"

"I still want him," I mumble without thinking, my heart speaking for me.

"Then make him work for it, Malisa. Don't just give up, but don't give in to him too easily, either. If Apollo loves you like I think he does, he'll give you what you need just to keep you. Lord knows he can afford it with the two billion dollars sitting in his bank account."

One bushel of advice down, and only God knows how many more to go.

I drop back on my hands and roll my head on my neck. Tension steadily rises, along with the uncomfortableness of this conversation that I didn't want to have with my mother. She's about to find out why her daughter hasn't been home. I don't want to see the disappointment in her eyes.

"I said I still want him, mama, not that I'm taking him back. Being with him for one night nearly cost my everything."

My heart lost it all.

"I know that's how you feel now, baby girl. But even if you had Apollo for one night or one eternity, the love of our lives has a way of making us change our minds, and it doesn't mean he'll give up on you just because you've given up on him. I wouldn't count him out just yet, either. From what I *heard* from just the short conversation between you two, he's doing things that he normally doesn't do, and he's doing them for *you*. He seems like the kind of man that gets what he wants when he decides it's the right time for him to have it, too. And I doubt if obstacles will keep him from what he wants. I can tell that just by looking at him. But if you don't want him, all you have to do is say the word. Now…"

She pauses, to grip my hands tightly in hers and pull me face to face with her. Her eyes aren't filled with disappointment or judgment like I expected them to be.

"I'm going to cook, Malisa, since I'm hungry and you're still in the bed. Blake will cook if we don't, and nothing he makes will be edible. You take all the time you need to get ready. I got a ski suit that'll fit you if you decide to take a walk later, if you want it. You will, because Apollo will insist on taking a walk. Privacy is nonexistent around here."

Her observation of the 'having one's space' shortage pulls a giggle from me, and I never said Apollo was worth two billion dollars.

"How do you know he's wealthy?"

My family is already starting to smother me, with love.

"The internet is available to everyone, not just the young people," she snipes.

I giggle.

God, what's with the giggling?

"You're forty-five, mama, not old. But if you can work a computer so well, how about you track my packages for me? My new, *clean* clothes should be arriving today, or I'll be walking around naked at work tomorrow. I'll take you up on that ski suit for later and the use of your washer and dryer." I'll need the walk, even if Apollo doesn't.

"I've already washed your clothes that were in your duffel bag. I got them after Blake picked your lock last night. We both wanted to make sure you were okay. They're in the top drawer of your dresser under the window. Nice dresses, by the way. And your new, *clean* clothes came a few minutes before I came up. They're outside your door. Apollo brought them up."

I shake my head and laugh. I should've known she'd be standing right beside Blake when he broke in my room last night. The Apollo I've gotten to know this weekend would've insisted on bringing up my clothes when I couldn't step in and stop him.

Lydia's fingers begin to fiddle with mine. "I told Apollo that Blake was in here with you before I opened the door, by the way. And then, I told him that him Blake is your brother by choice, not blood. Apollo wasn't happy about any of it, completely jealous." Then she breaks out in guilty snickers.

I guess I'm not crazy; Apollo was jealous, which only makes me laugh harder.

"My own mother set me up while most of the family is here, giving them something to speculate about. Did they ever go home last night?"

"I set Apollo up. You and Blake just got caught in the crossfire, but I don't see any bullet holes in either of you, so I think you're both good. Yes, the family went home. But everyone came back as early as they could, after getting their kids off to school, to see the fireworks here. Big mouth Blake told everyone about the two men who would be showing up this morning."

"You are ruthless, mama! I'm starting to believe daddy when he claims your father was a mob boss. I should've just called home yesterday, instead of coming here."

She raises one eyebrow and tilts one corner of her mouth up, a devilishly grin if I've ever seen one. "You have no idea how ruthless I can be, baby girl. And my father was—"

"Where are the eggs, Mama O?" Blake yells up the stairs, interrupting.

Several loud denials of eating anything he cooks if he can't even find the eggs follow right behind Blake's yell. Uncle Tommy is the loudest of the bunch that's probably running from the formal dining room attached to the left side of the kitchen, wanting to remain living.

My mother releases my hands to stand up. "I have to go, baby girl. Blake knows what he's doing. Threatening to burn my house down will get him what he wants. *Breakfast*!"

I flop backwards on the bed and let the expanding amusement in my chest rise out of my mouth. "Mama, you have completely spoiled and ruined that man for any woman."

"That's her problem," Lydia chirps back then bends over me and pecks me on the forehead. "I love you, baby girl."

"I love you too."

She moves toward my bedroom's doorway. I follow her into the hallway littered with three big boxes lined against the wall, which I have no hope of carrying into my room. Instead, I bend at the waist and peel the tape back on the first one, and then take the first pair of whatever is fit for Colorado's weather off the top. It happens to be an off-the-shoulder brown, crochet sweater, black skinny jeans, and brown wedge-heel boots. What I'm missing is a coat that can keep the wind and cold from molesting me, but that's nothing a trip to town or the coat to my mother's ski suit won't cure.

I stand up to take my haul back into my room. Apollo appears at the bottom of the steps, in the corner of my eye. I turn my head and get the full effect of him waiting just for me. My feet glue themselves to the floor, giving him the chance to roam his eyes over me, with my stupid heart calling out to him.

The next seven months are going to be hell.

"Sweetheart, how long is it going to take you to get ready?" he asks quietly.

I realize that his time here with me is taking away from his hectic schedule in Utah, and then I realize that's he's here *with* me, just when he shouldn't be. Were we ever going to get things right between us?

"Ah… I… I'm…" I realize I'm stammering like an idiot. "I'll be down ASAP, Apollo…" I clear my throat. "I mean, Mr. Ford."

He grins.

"Calling me Apollo is fine… Malisa."

Suddenly, it's weird to hear the correct pronunciation of my name from his mouth.

I wasn't sure what was okay between us anymore.

"Fine, Apollo, I'll…" I point behind me. "…go get ready."

He cocks his head to the side. "Hurry up."

I spin away, stumble into my room, then shut the door behind me. There's no point in locking it, but I have to press my back to it, needing a stable link to this earth and time for my knees to become steady again. I decide the next seven months in Apollo's employ are going to be worse than hell. I push off the door to drop my clothes on the bed then take my clothes off. Leaving them in a puddle on the tan carpet, I enter my bathroom and take as quick a shower as possible.

Everything is just where I left it in the bathroom, too bad the same can't be said about my love life. Twenty minutes pass before I've dressed, flat-ironed my hair, applied a layer of mascara and gloss to my face and my clothes to my body. I like what I see in the full-length mirror that's sitting in the corner of my room between the window beside my bed and the dresser pushed against the wall. After a quick clean up, I open the bedroom door, as ready as I'll ever be, with an audience.

The aroma of searing bacon assaults my nose, making my stomach grumble. I descend the stairs, and stop dead in my tracks. Apollo and Derek are sitting on each side of the great room on my mother's Victorian furniture. They stand up. I groan, and lean against the edge of the end of the staircase's banister.

"My mother is going to kill everybody."

Lydia laughs, from behind Derek, who was sitting with his back to the wide doorway leading into the kitchen. "*I* put them in here, Malisa, where the *guests* go. Calm down before you have them thinking I'm a raging monster most of the time."

I scoff, bravely and disrespectfully, because I'm standing several feet away and out of the reach of her open palm. "You are a raging monster when it comes to *this* room." And her family.

"That's because it wasn't for you and Blake to play in and destroy, baby girl."

"Or sit in," Blake adds, materializing behind her, with a platter of bacon pressed to his chest, which is now wrapped in a hunter green sweater above khaki pants and camel-colored boots.

He's dressed almost identical to Derek, who's wearing his aviator's jacket over his sweater with leather patches.

Lydia cranes her neck to look back at Blake. "Is that all the bacon I cooked?"

He grins and stuffs a piece in his mouth. "Yep. I'm saving it from Uncle Tommy."

She smirks. "You're saving it *for* yourself. You have to share."

"Why, Mama O? You'll just give it to me if I ask for it, and Pop's off pork. Lisa Poo is a model now, so she can't have any either, and I'm a big man."

"What about the rest of us, Blake?" Chrysalis asks in her sultry tone that meshes well with her femme fatale personality and looks. She's well aware that she's entering into the middle a middle of a battle while walking up behind Blake.

She's also beautiful, single, childless, and a much shorter and softer version of my father, with big, bouncy curls that reach to the arch in her back, wide curvy hips, and a small everything else clothed in a black, velvet cat suit and stiletto knee boots. Derek's head turns to acknowledge my aunt and never turns back around. My eyes roam to Apollo, wondering if he's enjoying Chrysalis' beauty, too. But his eyes are stuck to my face, and I can't look away.

Apollo reaches over, lets his fingers find the edge of his white-bubble coat resting on the back of the couch, and then motions with the tilt of his head toward the front door beside me. It takes strength that I have to dig deep to find just to turn away from him. It takes even more to move towards where he wants me to be, outside, where we'll get the only privacy available. I palm the knob. Another hand palms mine, before I can open the door.

I look up into Apollo's face, his eyes aglow with indignance. I've insulted him again, just by not letting him open the door for me.

Well, if he wants to open it that badly. I remove my hand from beneath his and step back, happy to avoid another argument that will have him hopping the next thing smoking back to Utah. I'm conflicted about how much damage he is doing to me by just being in the same room, but I still want him near. My world just isn't right when he isn't close. He smiles, the turmoil in his eyes fading away as he opens the door, allowing frigid air to rush us. I wonder if it is really this easy to make this man happy, while hugging myself to keep the cold at bay.

"Thank you," he says softly beside me.

"I think that's my line, Apollo."

I step out onto the porch then walk to the opposite end, where there's wicker rocking chairs and benches to choose from. I stop at the railing that's circling the porch, and look out into the open twenty acres surrounding my parents' house. The same cars that were hogging the driveway yesterday are back, along with a black truck with extended cab parked at the end of it. I would rather count the cars than have the talk that's incoming. Whether Apollo wants me back or not, both could prove to be disastrous for me, more so for my heart. But I put my big girl panties on and wait for Apollo to be the first to speak, intending to be fine with whichever way this conversation goes.

The air grows stiff as if it's waiting for something, or maybe it's just me waiting and I'm stiff. He closes the door back, gently, and then walks up behind me, his breath fanning the hair on my neck. His closeness alone is enough to keep me warm, and yet I shiver when it washes over me.

"I'm sorry." His soft baritone runs through me.

I tremble, again, as he drapes his coat over my shoulders. I pull it tight around me, letting his scent waft off the material into my senses.

"I think 'I'm sorry' is my line, too, Apollo. You know I didn't want you to leave Vegas or me at the store. I just wanted you to calm down, so you would hear me when I explained that I don't need to be taken care of. It's first nature to do it myself, if I can. I have done it for so long; it's all I know. Thank you for bringing the boxes up to my room. *That* I most certainly couldn't have done myself."

"It was my pleasure, Malisa. It's always been my pleasure to do anything for you, but I may have gotten too comfortable with doing things for you behind the scenes. To you, it may have felt like I was springing something on you that you aren't used to in Vegas. I shouldn't have sat back so long and loved you from a distance. Now, I get to regret getting angry with you and leaving you in Vegas for as long as I live. I won't do either again, if that's what you're worried about. But don't punish me for wanting to do things for you by telling me you can do everything for you yourself. It hurts."

"I realized too late that maybe I was hurting you, Apollo, but that was never my intention. I would have explained that if you had just waited for me. You're not the only one that got comfortable with doing things behind the scenes. Somehow, we got our wires crossed when we both stepped up. But I have to admit, you do the most serene and beautiful angry that I've ever seen."

That earns me a few laughs from him. The tension eases around us, and the world grows a little brighter and more beautiful, which means my happiness is tied to his. It probably always has been. All the more reason to fear losing him.

"If it makes things a little clearer between us, my Lisa. I have never met a woman like you who didn't want everything handed to them. I didn't calm down until I got here this morning and knew you were safe for myself." He exhales. "I have something else to confess."

"Well, I know you don't have my phone because I have it, so what could you have possibly done now?" I jab.

"Turn around and look at me, and I'll tell you."

I turn, placing my ass against the railing and spreading my feet wide apart to brace myself for whatever he is about to say before making eye contact with him. It's sizzling. More warmth swamps me. I no longer need to hug myself or Apollo's coat to keep warm. The cold air is suddenly a welcomed caress on whatever heated skin it can reach, mostly my face. It takes everything within me not to wrap my arms around Apollo, just to be closer. I'm not sure what he's about to say, and touching him may be the last thing he wants me to do, after he's said his piece.

He steps closer anyway, making me crane my neck to look up at him. "I've been sleeping at your apartment since Sunday night."

I blink.

That's all he had to confess? I take immense comfort in him being in my space, even if he didn't want me in his. He had to be missing me as much I missed him.

"You could've gotten in trouble for that, even if you have a key to my place, Apollo, which you still have because I never got it off the table in Vegas. You didn't have my permission to be there."

His hands drop down on my hips, making my breath rattle in my lungs.

"I wouldn't get in trouble if I owned the building and was keeping an eye on my tenant's place," he adds with a smug grin. "It's perfectly within my landlord's rights to make sure your home is secure while you're gone."

My knees wobble beneath me, and my eyes begin to bulge out of my head.

His smile evaporates. "But seriously, your apartment was all I had of you in Utah at the time, and I wanted it." His eyes lower to my mouth, distracting me. "Your smell was everywhere. It was as much torture as it was comforting."

"My smell should've been everywhere, Apollo, because it's *my* apartment," I whisper, and then, his words sink in. "Did you just say you bought my building?" I think my body registered what he said before my mind did, and I'm still not sure if I heard him right.

Chapter Thirteen

"Yes, I bought your building. I counted on your landlord being tired of maintaining thirty apartments after twenty years and greed helped, as well. I approached him with cash for the building on good faith that he'll take care of the switching of the names on the deed. If he doesn't, who gives a shit right now? But I think he cleared out of his apartment the same day."

"When did you buy the building?"

His forehead dips, until it's flush with mine. "Monday. I spent two hours of my day at the bank, waiting for them to count a million dollars, while they tried to talk me out of walking out of there with cash. Banks can't use the money to extend credit to suckers if it's in my briefcase, but I can't sleep *or* work without you near. It was stupid enough to tell you to stay in Vegas another night just because I was angry, but I didn't want to say something stupid while I was there, so I left. We both know that didn't work out well. When you didn't follow me home, I was still too angry to call you and beg you to come home. So I called the hotel instead, to check on you. You were still there. I went to the one place I knew you'd come back to, if not me... *your* home."

I giggle. "That didn't work out well either, did it?"

"No," he says promptly. "I stayed at your place, hoping you would ignore my instructions and show up before work Monday. You didn't. I called the hotel, again. You were still there. I knew I'd lost you, and tried to accept that you may have been right about us risking everything we already had to be together, so I tried go to work as usual Monday morning. I couldn't focus. I wanted to be wherever you were, except I still had to deal with the stupid meetings that I'd put off till Monday. I stayed at the office long enough to call my clients and investors just to cancel, again, before I went back to your apartment where I ran into your landlord first in the hallway. He was looking at me like I was going to steal something. I didn't like it, so, on a whim, I decide to buy the building."

I can imagine Mr. Crowder limping down the hallway of my floor on his bad knee that detests cold weather to get a good view of the man he'd never seen in the building before. I shake my head and try not to laugh.

"That had to be weird, since Mr. Crowder is a black man. But I highly doubt you were experiencing reversed racism, just him being protective. But apparently, everyone has a price."

Apollo chuckles dryly. "We do, and it's safe to say that I haven't made any money since you left Friday, but that's not what I care about most right now. We need to get to know each other, Malisa. I told you I wasn't letting you go, and I meant it. I told you if you needed more time to live, I'd give it, and I meant that, too. But you have to choose where we go from here because I'd glue you to my side if it was up to me, but I don't think that'll work for you. I hate that we don't know each other well enough to predict the other's mood outside of the office or what to do about them, even after working together for years."

My eyes drift closed, heartrate picking up speed. He'd put the burden on me to decide our fate, and it is a much heavier load than I've ever had to carry before. I've never loved anyone like this before, wholeheartedly. My heart clanging inside my chest like there's a major emergency somewhere is giving me an idea of what to do though. Follow its lead, by taking this opportunity to be back in Apollo's arms and running with it.

I don't think he needs a crystal ball to know my mood right now or what to do about it. My body is humming, and my mind fuzzy. He's standing too close for me to think straight and not want him. There's no way in hell we're going to be able to work together if I have immediate access to his body during working hours. Some days never stop at Global Ford Enterprises. I'm not sure if I won't try tricking him into the copy room beside his office, just to take what I want from him.

Just keep talking, Malisa. You're not in danger of taking anything from him if you're running your mouth, I think.

"You got one thing right, Apollo. We both reacted wrong Sunday. I really wasn't trying to hurt you *or* make you feel useless, but some things are just hard to change. Being independent is one of them, and I like it, which may be hard for you to believe after the type of women you've dated. I'm not saying all socialites are gold diggers, but I didn't think you'd ever see me as someone you could date either. And I didn't come back to Utah because you'd broken my heart. It had nothing to do with you doing things for me. You don't have to go out of your way, either. That was what I wanted to explain to you. I came here because I thought it was already too late to explain or get to know you better, and I needed to regroup. If I had come back to work Monday, I would've just cried all day. We both wouldn't have gotten anything done."

Apollo's hands slide from my hips to my waist. The physical contact, even with my sweater between our skin, rocks my world on its axis. My hands grab for his forearms, looking for an anchor to his world, since mine had flipped upside down.

"Look at me, my Lisa."

I open my eyes, slowly. They're weighted down with desire, which is threatening to overwhelm me. I get the urge to strip him of his clothes right here on the front porch. Looking into Apollo's eyes flooded with craving isn't making it any easier to resist it either. I'm warm enough to make love to him, right now, outside, but we have bigger problems like figuring out how not to kill one another as a couple.

"Do you still need to regroup, sweetheart?" he asks, while I try to cool down, mentally and physically.

"God yes. Just looking at you makes me scatterbrained, and I can't figure out what to do next to save us both from each other. All I know is I want you, even when I know it'll cost me dearly to lose you for any reason. That is still my main concern."

He smiles down on me, reminding me of the sunlight that nourishes my mother's plants. They could live without the light, but their growth would suffer tremendously. Apollo and I need to grow, and I need him to be my sunlight. My heart just refuses to let him go.

"Then let me save us," he whispers.

I grin, needing his help more than I ever had anyone's, to keep us together. "Take your best shot, Apollo."

"We stay here for another few days. It's what you need, love, after being away for so long. It's what your family needs after not seeing you, which is my fault. What better way to get to know someone than to be around the people that molded and shaped them? I just need to know if I'll be sharing rooms with Derek."

I begin to stare at him as if he's grown two heads. "Apollo, first off, I didn't take you for being suicidal. My mother, alone, will eat us alive. We won't have any time together, not to mention privacy, and you still have a business to run. Second, Derek is here because he only wanted to make sure I was okay. I explained to him yesterday that you had broken my heart and I just couldn't be anything more than a friend to him."

Apollo begins to laugh, and I think I've eased his mind about Derek's presence here.

"I don't know one single man that would settle for being just your friend when you're as beautiful as you are inside and out."

"Well, that's not my fault is it?"

"It sure isn't. But I have to ask, are you ready to go back to Utah because you want to get in my pants, my Lisa?"

"You're damn straight I want to get in your pants. I haven't done a tenth of the things I wanted to do to your body yet, and I have years of *not* getting into your pants to make up for."

"Same here, and we will. But we tried making love before dating, remember? How about we try dating before making love this time?"

I yelp, "What? That doesn't make any sense. Do you know how long I've been waiting to get in your pants? So long, I got tired of waiting and got a damn makeover to attract someone else. There's no way in hell I'm giving up your body, Apollo. You're just going to have to get to know me in between making love to me."

He throws his head back and laughs at my desperation. I'd find it funny too, if it wasn't *my* desperation that he was laughing at. Finally, his mirth winds down.

"Do you know how refreshing it is to know someone who just wants me for my body? But I wish you'd take my gifts, too. You're the only woman I know who I want to have both... along with my heart."

"I've been waiting on your heart, Apollo. But can we negotiate about the gifts? I take enough of your money from you just by working for you."

His smile vanishes. "No, we can't negotiate. You earn your paycheck, and whatever I do for you extra makes me happy, or I wouldn't do it."

I smile stupidly. I'm not supposed to be this happy about someone wanting to do things for me, but I am. It's the ultimate proof that he truly cares, but I need his body more than his gifts. "So, you're just going to take in this relationship? Not give me one thing that *I* want out of it?"

He leans in until his mouth is only inches from mine. "If your idea of 'just going to take in this relationship' means giving you everything I think you deserve, then yes, I'm just going to take in this relationship." And then, his mouth is on mine before I can bargain some more.

That's one way to shut me up.

The pressure of his lips against mine is enough to cook the air around me. His tongue tangling with mine is enough to make every fine hair on my body stand on end. A hard pole emerges between my thighs, stroking the most sensitive part of me there, while pressing against my pelvis. My hips grind against his on their own.

Apollo moans in my mouth then sucks my tongue deeply into his. It feels the same as being taken by him, which rockets my body's need to cum up to much higher than I can stand while being fully-clothed. When he tugs gently on my bottom lip with his teeth, goosebumps rise along my arms inside his jacket as if I'm cold, but I'm burning up inside. I tilt my head back and groan, with my eyes shut tightly.

Desire clanging just as loudly inside me as my heart is. I'm feeling too much, and I need relief. He releases my lip, pulls my hips into his, trapping his erection and my hardened nipples between us and torturing me.

"Fuck! Apollo, I need you, sweetheart," I hiss against his mouth.

"You got me, sweetheart."

I softly nip at his chin with my teeth and pull him even closer until his chest melds with mine.

"No, Apollo, I need you inside me."

His arms slide inside the jacket, around my waist, and begin to massage my spine.

"No, my Lisa, we're going to do this right and get to know one another. I'm going to make you accept the world from me before I give you what you want the most from me."

"You, Apollo. Just you."

"It's not just me, baby. I'm a whole package, and the things I want to do for you are the most important part. It's what makes me the man I want to be."

He wants to be a provider. This is as important to him as the air he breathes.

"And that's why you were so angry in Vegas because you thought I was rejecting the most important part of you?"

"Yes. So, I'm going to give you time to decide if you can compromise for me. If you can't, I'll understand and I'll get out of your way. I hope you decide to let me do whatever I want to for you. Because I can't give you the fairytale life with castle, princes, and princesses if you don't let me."

"That was a low blow, Apollo," I say patronizingly, with a grin on my face. "You're using the things I want the most from you to get what you want. I knew you were a tease, but I didn't want to believe it."

"I'm a businessman," he says arrogantly, while grinning back. "Giving you everything that you want so I can get what I want is the name of my game. Waiting for it just makes the win even greater, baby."

"You'll spoil her if you do that," Uncle Tommy warns from behind Apollo.

Apollo pecks me on the nose. "That's the plan, Mr. Owens."

"Call me, Tommy. Frank is the old guy."

The little privacy that Apollo and I had is gone. I groan and purse my lips. Staying here with him *and* my family is going to be an even bigger nightmare than I thought. I'd rather run his company single-handedly than be subjected to my family's nosiness.

Apollo steals a kiss from my lips before backing away. "You sure she isn't already spoiled? I've never seen her pout before." The absence of his arms is felt more and more with each step he takes.

Tommy leans against the edge of the opened doorway that he'd managed to sneak out of, with a grin on his face and his arms crossed over his lean chest. He dips his head at me and cocks a slightly bushy eyebrow.

"Apollo, that woman is half Lydia's, half Frank's, a walking contradiction that you're trying to tie yourself to. They taught her to spoil *herself* rotten because nothing in this world is free. I'm going to start praying for you *now*, my brother. But for now, if you two want anything to eat, I advise that you get in here now because Blake is *not* giving up this bacon. Next, he'll have the eggs and the toast, and we'll be eating each other. Blake gets his way, no matter whose house he's at."

Apollo stops reversing to look back at my uncle. "Are you kidding me?"

"Not even in the damn slightest," he deadpans, and that's about as serious as Tommy gets.

Tommy pushes off the doorway and reenters the house. When Apollo extends a hand to me, I push off the railing, and take it in mine. He turns sideways then drops my hand, to drape it around my hips and haul me side-to-side with him. When we walk inside the house, only then does he allow me to step away, so he can close the door behind us. I drape his coat on the back of the couch beneath the front windows, where it came from.

Derek is still standing and eye-fucking my aunt Chrysalis, while the battle of the pork is still raging in the doorway between the kitchen and the living room. Blake is still the sole possessor of the platter.

He points a piece of bacon at my aunt. "Same for you, Aunt Chrys. If I ask for it, you'll give it to me. Why bother with the whole argument we're having?" Then he pulls the platter closer to his chest, by enclosing it completely in the arm wrapped around the edge of it.

Chrysalis throws her hands up in the air and rolls her eyes heavenward. "He's a twenty-six-year-old brat, plain and simple, Lydia."

Lydia scoffs beside her, and waves a hand between them. "And we all equally share in the blame for that, Chrys. Now give me the plate, Blake." She reaches out for it.

He turns sideways. "But, Mama O, I need it. You know I don't eat this well at home and I'm single. Have some pity."

Derek begins to laugh then takes a hurried seat on the couch, his ability to stand giving out under the weight of his hilarity. Even Apollo laughs at a pleading Blake. Lydia tosses her hands in the air and blows air heavenward, as well. Chrysalis spins on her heels and vanishes into the kitchen, with Lydia following closely behind her and shaking her head. Blake looks at me, with his bright blues and a wide grin on his face, having won the war.

I point at Blake and look sideways at Apollo.

"This is *his* family," I say dryly. "I'm just black and the biological daughter."

Apollo grabs my pointer finger and pulls me in his arms in front of everyone. "I have all the bacon you want, love."

I lean close to whisper in his ear. "It's your sausage that I'm interested in, Mr. Ford."

He pecks me on the nose and strokes a stray lock of hair laying across my forehead. "In due time, love, I got you. You are so not like other women, my Lisa. I have so much more to offer you."

"No, she's not," Blake says, suddenly standing in front of us, with a whirlwind of emotions snapping in his eyes. "She deserves the best of everything, and I, as Sheriff Powers, will make sure she gets it." Then he extends the platter of bacon to me, after identifying himself in an underhanded way. I suspect he's issuing a warning for Apollo, who raises an eyebrow.

I'm more surprised that Blake offered me his food. "You're actually going to give me some of your food? You usually steal mine."

"And if you tell anybody that I gave you some, I'm putting you back on the no-fly list at the airport."

"Seriously, Blake!"

I never knew he'd taken me off, and he's already threatening to put me back on it. Like I said, he's a harmless bully, and I his helpless victim.

Chapter Fourteen

Derek sinks toward to the loveseat, holding his chest with one hand and guiding his way down with the other, before laughter rockets out of his mouth.

"No-fly list, Malisa! Tell me..." he struggles to speak between deep chuckles, "...your brother is joking, right?"

Apollo frowns.

I sigh. "No, Derek, he's not joking because he's an—"

"Hey!" Blake hollers around a mouth full of bacon. "I'm getting called an ass after offering you my food? Now take it before I change my mind."

I grab a piece off the platter before he does just that.

Blake spins around on the heel of his boots, grumbling under his breath, "Sisters! Such a pain in my ass."

"Mama!" I yell, "Blake's cussing!"

He spins back around and snatches the piece of bacon from my hand, which I should've eaten before indulging the childish need to tattle in good fun.

Then he tosses it back on the platter and stands before me, with his massive chest heaving and an extremely irritated look on his face.

"I know why you tried to get me in trouble, Malisa. It's because I'm white and adopted."

I step out of Apollo's arm to stop in front of Blake. I stand up on tiptoe and kiss him on the jaw. It's the only thing that stops the rant he always goes off on whenever he doesn't get his way, or wants us to think that he's feeling like an outcast. I step back to Apollo's side and lean into him.

"By the way, Blake, officially, you're not adopted. We just choose to love you."

He grins and offers me another piece of bacon. Derek succumbs to another round of chuckles. Apollo's forehead creases with wrinkles. I don't have to be in the office to know when something is worrying him, but I decide to get to the bottom of whatever it is after we find some more time to ourselves.

For now, I refuse Blake's offer with a shake of my head, while snickering. "You're a damn Indian-giver, Blake. Keep. It."

He shrugs, while eyeing the meat in his hand, and then he bites it before walking away, going to probably steal more breakfast items from the kitchen to go with the platter of bacon, which he'll munch on all day long.

Apollo watches him leave, then looks down at me grimly. "He's a brat."

Derek laughs harder. With the tilt of my head toward the couch, I motion for us to do something that I've only done twice in my life, sit down in the great room.

Once Apollo has settled beside me, with his arm wrapped around my waist, he asks, "How long has Blake been in your life?"

I shake my head and feign a frustrated sigh.

"Since he was seven. His parents invited mine to their yearly charity function for cerebral palsy, since my father's a pediatrician. They started talking about their kids. My mother found out that Ashley and Martin had a child born with the disorder at birth and didn't survive, and that they were leaving Blake with anyone that would take him, whenever they needed or wanted to take a trip. The au pair they'd shipped from England... well, I guess that makes her a governess, but she's still a nanny to me, got tired of raising Blake and quit when he was five. Lydia offered to babysit him, essentially offering him another family. Ashley took her up on it, not knowing my parents any better than you would a can of paint, or if we were a bunch of axe-murderers. Fortunately, for Blake, we're not. I wonder about my mother sometimes, though. She's nothing to play with, but he's been tormenting me ever since."

Apollo looks off, into the kitchen, where Blake disappeared to. "You two are really close then?"

"We were, about as close as my mother finding us in bed together was, without ever being romantically involved. But I haven't seen or talked to him since he had an argument with his parents after he graduated high school and wanted to go in the army to pay for college. His parents suddenly wanted him close. I guess since he wasn't a burden anymore, they thought he'd join them in their lifestyle, continuing the dynasty of Powers that have reigned in Arrow for generations and opened most of the ski resorts that are known worldwide. I'm sure that's how he got the position as Sheriff at twenty-six. But they screwed up and let Lydia and Frank get their hands on Blake first. He's just as independent as I was raised to be... when he isn't making us love on him that is. The only way to stop him from talking about he's white and adopted is to kiss him on the cheek. You should see how arrogant he looks when my mother and I *both* do it together."

I see Derek sit up from the corner of my eye. "And you're jealous, Apollo."

Apollo's eyes snap to Derek. Suddenly, the tension that was missing between the two, when they found Blake and I in the bed together, is flooding the room. I sit up beside Apollo, whose expression is dark, his eyes imitating daggers.

"Yes, I am jealous, Derek. I should've been the one sleeping with her last night."

I swallow loudly. Somehow, I knew Blake and my mother's actions would come back to bite me in my ass, which is not damn fair. Why isn't it biting them in theirs, too?

"You couldn't have wanted to sleep with her if you left her in Vegas this weekend," Derek responds before I can think of what to say to check the situation before it gets any worse, which it just did.

Derek shifts on the loveseat, placing his spine flat against the back of the chair and crossing his arms. The air pulls tight around us. The cold creeps in from the outside.

Apollo leans forward, resting his elbows on his knees spread slightly apart. "Why are you even here?"

Derek shrugs. "Visiting my friend."

"Your friend!" Apollo's voice rises an octave. "You don't even know her, and you just wanted to date her four days ago. Now you're friends? Well, you can go home now. Malisa and I are fine and she has *me* to check on her." His ire rises right along with his tone.

I get even more worried. Apollo and Derek are big men, and I see no way of keeping them apart if the situation escalates anymore. This would be a good time for my family to be all up in my business, or for Officer Powers to show up. Even bratty Blake putting in an appearance with his platter of stolen bacon is alright with me.

Derek hardens his expression and leans forward, while working his jaw. "I settled for Malisa's friendship when I realized how much she was hurting over you. Even after meeting her just four days ago, I can see she's a good woman. You had four years to learn that, and still screwed it up. But no man can win against heartache for another man, unless he doesn't mind being a rebound. Since I like being first in a woman's affections, I learned my place in her life quickly and came to make sure she didn't spend all day and night crying over you. And while I hoped you saw what you were losing, now I hope you crash and burn, *jackass*!"

Apollo stares not at Derek but through him. "Jackass? I'm not surprised that you'd stoop low to name-calling since you slithered into Malisa's parents' home the minute I wasn't around."

"Apollo," I called worriedly. "He's didn't—"

"Are you calling me an opportunist?" Derek cuts me off then stands up.

Apollo gets to his feet. "I'm calling you a snake."

"Derek, you should leave," I say quickly before he can respond.

The argument wouldn't have started if he hadn't provoked Apollo, and I didn't see a satisfactory end to it or either man backing down anytime soon. I step in between them though Derek is several feet away, but I don't know how long that's going to last.

Derek reaches for his coat that's laying on the back of the chair he was sitting on, without taking his eyes off Apollo.

My mother walks into the room, to stand beside me. "Derek's my guest now, baby girl, and I'm only the one who raises hell in here fellows. Disrespect my house again and you're both out. Start getting along right now. You should take Apollo into the dining room, Malisa. Derek follow behind them… slowly."

Before I can ask my mother what she meant by Derek being her guest, she walks away.

Apollo reaches for my hand. "She's right, sweetheart. Even serpents have a purpose, and he should stay so he can see for himself that you have a man who isn't going anywhere no matter if I'm in the area or not."

Derek snickers under his breath, taking the jab well. I risk a glance at him. He winks. I get suspicious and take my first breath. Like I said, men are not worth the trouble. But I want Apollo, anyway.

A moving shadow on the floor snags my attention. I look up at a smirking Blake, lifting more bacon from the confiscated plate to his mouth, while he leans against the doorframe. Officer Powers is officially on duty. I blow him a kiss, for being willing to save my ass and my mother's furniture if shit got real in here between Apollo and Derek. I'm just not sure if Derek was ever going to let it get that far or if my mother's intervention wasn't timed. As soon as I catch her alone, I'm going to find out if it was, and if this argument was a setup, too.

Blake drops the bacon, to catch my blown kiss in one fist then palms his cheek before vanishing, again.

"Come and eat, everyone," my mother shouts, from the kitchen. "Everyone except Blake that is."

"Mama O, come on!" he whines, possibly standing right behind her and salivating over whatever she's transferring to a serving dish.

Derek waits for us to walk past, before he falls in line behind us, with me leading the way to the dining room. After passing over the threshold into the kitchen, where my mother bends down in front of a stainless-steel stove, removing biscuits from the oven, I veer to the left and walk through another wide doorway.

Everyone would normally be in the small breakfast room on the right side of the kitchen, seated around the custom-made, circular breakfast nook. However, everyone isn't in there. Most are already in the formal dining room, only my father and Tommy are missing, both probably in the den. I glance heavenward, at the huge chandelier with gold spider arms angling toward the high ceiling and burgundy lamps encasing the bulbs. I remember when I had the misfortune of getting caught swinging from one of the arms. Blake dared me a whole fifty cents to do it, which I thought was a lot of money at nine-years-old. So I did it, but didn't get the fifty cents.

The spanking I got in its place wasn't worth it either. Blake got one too for daring me, which is why he didn't pay me, and I didn't let him talk me into anything else after that. Luckily for him, the poo incident came a year earlier. What Blake tricked me into doing then shall never be spoken of.

I seat Apollo and Derek in the empty chairs one seat down from the head of the table, where my father and mother will sit, making sure

Derek is seated next to Chrysalis. Hopefully, her presence will keep him from provoking Apollo again.

Frank and Tommy enter the room. Neither is smiling, which is odd for Tommy.

Something isn't right.

Apollo's first visit is turning out to be more nerve-racking than doing several jobs at his company. My nerves rattle inside me, as I step back toward the hutch filled with dishes that we never eat out of. My father and uncle claim the narrow walkway between me and the dining room table and take their seats. Tommy will speak his mind, which doesn't amount to much when you don't know what will come from him next. My father hasn't had to deal with male visitors of mine, ever, so I don't have the faintest clue of what he'll do and say, period.

Frank grabs the empty seat at the head of the table. Tommy sits on his left, in front of Apollo but beside Derek. Luke is positioned beside Apollo, with the twins, Jen and Barbie, taking up the rest of the seats on the opposite end of the table from my father. My mother will take her husband's lap, like always, which leaves nowhere for me to sit.

I can always eat standing up, I muse, before I leave the room to help my mother haul breakfast platters, dinner plates, and utensils into the dining room. I stop beside her who is glazing the biscuits with butter, to pull dinner plates from the top shelf of the oak cabinet. I stretch up, but Blake appears behind me and grabs them first, setting them on the countertop filled with small kitchen appliances and ceramic jars.

"Take them in, Blake," Lydia says suddenly. "I need to speak with Malisa."

I sidestep, so Blake can switch out the platter of bacon for the dinner plates.

He nods, giving no customary back talk just to receive a smack upside the back of his head for it.

Oh God, something is definitely up, but at least my nerves can't get any more shaken.

Whatever is up, I'm in the middle of it, all by my lonesome.

"Follow me, baby girl," my mother demands.

She turns one hundred and eighty degrees then moves toward the closed pantry door. She goes in first and flips the switch. The room has always felt ominous to me because the single bulb above us has never cast that much light. Ominous is having triple the effect with anxiety pooling inside me. Then she signals for me to close the door behind us.

"What's is it, mama?"

"Are you okay? Your father heard the argument between Derek and Apollo, and I know him. He's not taking this well." *This* is new for all of us.

"I'm fine, mama. Apollo just—"

"Apollo is just jealous, Malisa. Derek gained some points with the family, for backing off when you told him to. But Apollo is not faring so well with his outburst of jealousy in the living room. It's typical of men in love, but that doesn't mean we like it. Jealous sometimes leads to other problems in a relationship."

Shit! I'll bet they're all reporting to each other on every move we make, too.

I swipe at my forehead wearily. "So you guys are a network of spies now?"

"Damn straight. When it comes to you, we're all ready to kill on command, if needed. Now, do us a favor and stick close to the house, for as long as Apollo's here. In case you're wondering, Derek's provoking him intentionally to see what he'll do."

"I knew you two were up to something. Why you would you do that to Apollo?"

"Because that's what investigators do, find out shit. So I hired him while you were upstairs talking to Apollo. Derek chose to do it for free since he can't stay for long. We both want to know if Apollo has any bad tendencies. I want them to show up today."

"Jesus, mama—"

"Jesus has nothing to do with this, Malisa. You live a whole state away from the safety of your family. Yes, Apollo loves you. That much I'm sure of, but that doesn't make him a good guy or the right guy for you, and Jesus rarely shows up when your children are in the company of a monster. That's why they have parents."

God, my whole family is overreaching and completely paranoid.

But at least Derek is being an asshat to Apollo for a reason, my mother's.

I take her hands in mine.

"Mama, Apollo's a good guy who wants to stay here for a few more days to get to know me. But I suspect he's wanting to let you all get to know him, too. A monster wouldn't do that if he could help it. They tend to isolate their women."

"I know, but listen, baby girl—"

"You guys have to trust me. I've lived at Apollo's side, literally, day in and day out, and he's never done or said anything out of the way to anyone. If he had said something about his feelings for me, we would've been together way before now. I know what I want. But even if Apollo and I are together to the end of time, I'm not staying away from my family anymore, so stop worrying."

Her fingers squeeze mine, and she smiles. I don't have to be a rocket scientist to know that her daughter being out of reach is what's worrying her the most.

"I trust you, love, and yes, it would be nice if you visited a lot more often. Hell, I'd have started visiting you as soon as you graduated and found a job in Utah, but Blake found his way back here first. You've always been good at taking care of yourself, but someone has to watch over Blake until he settles down. He puts up a good front, but he still hasn't found his place in this world yet, and he hates working and living in Colorado. I think it's too slow for him, and his parents are still trying to convince him to become one of them. They even pulled strings to get him the Sheriff position when the last one took ill in the middle of his term. Being a deputy starting out wasn't good enough for them. He feels somewhat obligated to stay here because they're his parents. I wish he'd tell them to kiss off already, but I'll stand by whatever decision you two make, and I'll be there when you make another one, whether good or bad."

"But you're not going to call off your dogs, are you?" I ask, sarcastically.

She trusts me, but she cares too much for us to ever just let us do things on our own.

She snickers evilly. "Hell no. We need to get back out there so I can figure out Apollo some more."

"*Figure out*," I shriek. This has gone too far. "You are *not* a spy, mama!"

She stops smiling, her hazel eyes diamond hard, suddenly dead serious. "Says you, Malisa. I'm whatever I need to be to make sure you're happy. That includes being an axe-murderer." And she's an eavesdropper, too.

"Why do I believe you?"

"Because you should. My father wasn't a mob boss, but he led a gang in Chicago and did whatever needed to be done for his family. My parents taught me to do the same before they both died in a drive-by, right after I met your father on a college campus. They both were too young to die from natural causes as I led you to believe. I was supposed to be taking some drugs to your father's friends when he asked me out. And then, I got pregnant with you. I'm sure you don't need those details, just that I moved here to Colorado before I had you, where my old life had next to zero chances to touch you. But it'll touch

Apollo if he isn't careful and you come home with one more broken heart."

Chapter Fifteen

I stare at my mother dumbfounded. I have a new respect for her, if it is even possible to respect her more. She'd left all she'd known to make a good life for me and someone else's child here, and she's still doing it even after we've grown up. I suspect I'll care for my children just as much and will try to circumvent whatever troubles they may have, if I can, however I need to.

"I never knew my grandfather was a thug. You could've told me. I would've understood. Everybody has beginnings and now I know where you got your edge from it."

"In that case, your grandmother was his bottom bitch, and God knows I hope you don't know what that means. You weren't supposed to know any of this until you were old enough to understand, Malisa. Your father wanted me to tell you way before now, so you didn't grow up sheltered. But who could grow up sheltered around Blake? That kid was a bad influence if I ever knew one."

"You are not lying there. I stuck my hand in dog poo because of him."

She giggles hard enough to make her shoulders and ample breasts vibrate under a black long-sleeve blouse topping her navy-blue slacks.

"You telling me the gritty details of your childhood wouldn't have been bad for me, mama, especially after dealing with Blake."

"It was hard enough living with my childhood myself. I would never have subjected you to the details of it when you were young," Lydia says sincerely.

"I understand, mama; I really do. Now, let's get back out there before something else happens. Daddy's in the dining room with

Apollo, and your husband doesn't look happy. Neither does Uncle Tommy. That's worrying all by itself."

She reaches behind me and pushes the door open. We walk in the direction of massive amounts of chatter migrating out of the dining room, filling up the kitchen. Even Apollo is laughing at something, his laughter taking up most of the space in the kitchen. Derek is listening intently to Chrysalis, who's thirty-eight, divorced, and probably explaining that she runs a bounty-hunting agency with her twin sisters, out of Spinley, a small but high-crime city only one county over. I realize these two have a lot of common, Derek being only two years younger than Chrysalis.

However, daddy seems to just be observing, as usual. Never the one to jump to conclusions, he takes his sweet time making decisions about everything. He's giving Apollo a chance to grow on him. My mother usually swings her axe first, and maybe give her unapologetic reasons for it later. If you have a problem with them, well, that's your problem. But she must be giving Apollo a chance to grow on her, too, for me, because her axe is still stuck in the chopping block and not being wiped down. I'm blessed to have the parents that were gifted to me. *Even if they are nosy as hell.*

I stop in the doorway and turn to Lydia beside me. "Thanks, mama."

She frowns by squishing up her button nose and furrowing her forehead. "For what?"

"For being you... and not swinging your axe yet."

She grins, deviously. "It's being sharpened as we speak, baby girl. Just in case."

I turn my head, or she'd slap me on the back of it if she saw me rolling my eyes. "Lord, this is going to be a few days to remember."

She snorts. "If Blake is here, damn straight it will be. He's two handfuls, and he doesn't care who knows it."

She leaves me to walk by Blake, who's sitting in front of the dishes, which he was left to carry into the dining room by himself. Apollo is being flanked on both sides by two of the biggest men in my family; Blake and my father. He doesn't seem to care that they're surrounding him, which shouldn't bother me much since he's massive himself at six feet three inches, but it does. I grow more so when my mother walks over to my father, to sit down sideways in his lap, as soon as he makes room for her to slide her short legs under the table. She's the smallest and most dangerous of the crew, even if Chrysalis is a bad ass in her own right.

After Tommy is finished cracking his latest joke, Apollo looks up at me, and then he stands up. "Come sit down, my Lisa. You haven't eaten anything."

I tilt my head to the side, waiting for him to reach me. I love him a little more for always seeming to think of me, even when I don't realize he's doing it or remember to appreciate it.

"Still keeping tabs on my digestive track, huh?"

"Always."

"But you're the guest, Apollo. I can eat standing up."

His feet move into the narrow walkway, bringing him to me and making the room grow eerily quiet. "I'm good, sweetheart. A gentleman doesn't leave his woman standing."

"I'll sit when you're done, Apollo. Deal?" I bargain, hoping he isn't going to make a big deal of who sits down in front of everyone in the room. They're watching us like hawks.

He shakes his head and reaches for my hand. "No deal, love. You can have my lap." Then he dips his head closer to mine. "I've missed you, and I need to make up for the time we spent apart this weekend."

My eyes stray to everyone else. Blake nods. My father winks. I sigh, feeling outnumbered. My next lesson in letting my man do something for me is already here. Since I've already been down this road, I go with the one less traveled.

"Fine, Apollo. You get your way, this time."

I let him guide me to his chair, where I mimic my mother's position in my father's lap on Apollo's. He reaches around my waist with one hand and for the forkful of fluffy scrambled eggs laying on his plate in front of me with the other. When he lifts it, the eggs wobble on the utensil, threatening to fall in my lap. I cup one palm under the fork automatically, toss the other behind his back, just as my mother is doing for my father who's always juggled her on his lap and eating. They've done this for as long as I've been alive at least.

Apollo guides the food to my mouth instead of his.

Lydia laughs behind me. "You're a quick learner, Malisa. I had to get a spoonful of hot mashed potatoes in my lap before I figured out to watch your father with food like a hawk. He refuses to get that I bought enough chairs so *everyone* would have somewhere to sit."

"My lap is your chair, sweetheart," my father says, before kissing her cheek quickly.

Tommy sniggers under his breath, the only warning you get before someone becomes the butt of his joke. "God knows your lap is big enough to sit everyone in here in it altogether, Frank. Luke's, too."

Getting in two butts for one of his jokes is common, too.

Someone snorts, and the room erupts with laughter.

My father rests his fork on the side of his plate, closes his eyes, and shakes his head. "Shut up, Tommy."

My uncle shrugs his slim shoulders and tries to stop laughing, but snorts break free from deep within his throat. "It's not my fault you're both are built like damn lumberjacks. God rest your dead mother's and father's souls."

My mother covers her mouth and turns toward me to hide her giggles.

139

My father sighs and grits his teeth. "They were your parents too, and for God's sake, shut... up... Tommy."

I barely notice when Blake gets up from the table suddenly, with Apollo's chest vibrating against my side. His quiet but manic laughter is making his arms shake and almost impossible for him to stab more eggs with his fork. I'm not interested in getting a lap full of anything, so I watch him closely.

"I love your family," says Apollo.

"Oh, they're a riot," I respond, with a smirk. "But it will get old to you when you become the butt of their jokes."

"That just means you're a part of the family, sweetheart."

"Now tell us about your family, Apollo," Blake demands suddenly from behind us.

The mirth rumbling through Apollo's body stops suddenly. He freezes in place, as if he's death warmed over, while staring down at his plate. I know immediately that this is a sore subject for him. But we all want to know about his origins, and he is going to have to open up. I start to stroke his back, hoping to give him reassurance that it's okay and he isn't alone, and wanting to kill Blake for ruining the good time that Apollo was having.

I swear Blake timed it perfectly, as if he knew when the mention of family would come up. I'm sure it would have, at some point. But, did he have to be the one to bring it up and kill the mood for everyone?

I glare back at him. He's now standing in the back entrance to my father's den, eating a slice of bacon casually, as if he didn't just become a major ass and killjoy for everyone. Or at least for me and Apollo. The turning of Apollo's head draws my attention.

When I look down, he's looking back, with the guiltiest of expressions on his face.

"I don't have any family," he says softly.

He seems to be confessing. I feel terrible for him, and can't imagine not having any family behind me. I grow to appreciate the presence of mine even more, faults and all, maybe not Blake's presence for a while though. He seems to be going out of his way to put Apollo on the hot seat.

"It's okay, Apollo," I whisper. "Not having family is nothing to be ashamed about."

His head drops. "Yeah, well, for the most part, I don't care that my parents dumped me in an orphanage in Montreal, Canada… when I was two. I migrated to the United States and ended up in Utah, where I went to college, after a series of foster homes that never adopted me as one of their own in any way."

I wonder how could someone feel unloved most of their life and still become successful. Apollo looks off, seeming to drift mentally, while picking at the food on his plate, with a captive audience made of everyone in the room waiting for him to pick up where he'd left off.

"When I hired Malisa, she became the only family I wanted around, and I tried to make her a permanent, solitary member of it without her permission." Then he smiles, with one side of his mouth, and I've never felt so loved, and that's saying something when I've had the Owens standing behind me since I'd formed my first memory.

Apollo shuffles the eggs on the fork with one hand then guides it to my mouth. "I finally met someone that I needed more than I needed to make something of myself, proving to the people who dumped me as a child and took half-hearted stabs at raising me that I had worth."

His eyes meet mine. The emotions swirling in his dark orbs grab something deep within me, holds on firmly, and makes the world shift around me. I could actually see the love he has for me, and it's a heady sight.

141

"And then I lost you in Vegas, my Lisa, and lost everything that really mattered. So yes, I followed you here to tell you that face to face and whatever else anyone wants to know about me. You're the reason my parents not raising me themselves doesn't hurt like it used to, and I don't care if I don't ever make another cent at my company. All of that will never be as important as making you happy."

Apollo's words hit me right in the throat. Emotions well up there and the backs of my eyes begin to burn. My hand lifts to pinch his chin lightly between my fingers. Then I tilt it up so his mouth will be in place for my lips that are dipping to touch down on his softly. I'm seeking comfort from him instead of giving it to him, but he'd rocked me, again, from the inside out. I need to touch something that isn't rocking with me. Then I back away slowly. I'm not much for public displays of affections, but I needed to do that.

Blake appears behind Apollo and tosses a blue manila folder on the table between the platter of the bacon he'd confiscated and Apollo's plate. "They did love you, Apollo. You should read that when you get a chance."

Apollo and I both stare down at the folder. It quickly becomes my version of poisonous snakes, with fangs in the form of words and Blake's deed, which was sinking into me. I look back at Blake, who's reversing to his corner in the doorway of my father's den, as if he's getting out of harm's way.

"Where did you get this?" I snarl. "When?"

"I had a detective who owed me a favor working around the clock since Sunday on this. When you disappeared, I needed to know who was with you last and if a serial killer was following my sister home to her family."

I glance at my mother. She looks back, unashamed. But my father glimpses at Tommy, both wearing a guilty look so much like the one on Apollo's face before he revealed where he'd come from. Tommy looks at Derek. The network of spies have gone too far with invading Apollo's life. This has probably made him feel unwelcomed here. I feel as if my choices in life aren't trusted. I stab the folder with a trembling fingertip.

"This is an invasion of privacy! Blake, you had no right to do this. Apollo's parents have nothing to do with me going missing, which I wasn't." I scan the room including each person in the room in my raging glare.

Apollo grabs my finger and moves it to his lips. "They did the right thing, sweetheart, even if I didn't really want to track down my parents yet. At least Blake had the nerve to do what I never could, find out who they. I convinced myself that I didn't need them in my life if they were still alive, and it was a constant battle. But when you came into my life, I knew it wasn't true. If I were your family, I'd look into everyone's background that was around you the time you'd gone missing, too. I may have known you were safe at the hotel, but your family doesn't know me from a hill of beans, and I'm not surprised that they didn't take my word."

I feel the urge to ball up the manila folder and throw it away. Whatever's in it, I want to hear right out of Apollo's mouth. My family should've waited for him to tell us, too.

"We need to talk, Apollo," I mumble, needing more to apologize for Blake's behavior privately than discuss the contents of the file.

He flops back in his chair. "Yes, we do. Where is there to go so we aren't interrupted?"

My father's shed outside the French doors of the dining room comes to mind immediately, and Apollo having to leave soon to go back to work does, too.

"I'll show you, but I need to change my clothes first. It's cold out there," I mention quietly grabbing the file. Fury is flowing through me, but I force a comforting smile to my lips for Apollo's sake.

Chapter Sixteen

My mother reaches over my knees to seize my hand and grab my attention before I can get to my feet. "That ski suit is on my bed, Malisa, with the fur-lined boots and matching hat that go nicely with it. I'm sure you have T-shirt in one of those boxes upstairs."

She lets my hand go. "See you when you get back from the shed, and please put on lots of clothing. It's really cold out there."

I glance down at Apollo and snap, "See what I mean?"

He starts to vibrate with quiet amusement, again, while standing up behind me. "I envy you for having so many people that genuinely care for you. I didn't find that until I met you."

I start to think that I attract orphaned men, then I lift my chin and squint my eyes at Apollo. "You don't know that yet."

"Even if my parents do care for me, I know you did when you blasted me for spending money on you without checking with you first. I didn't know how to take that until now. Anyone that cares for you wants you to keep what you've worked for and give you what they have to go with it. I haven't had anyone in my life to teach me that before you. Now let's go get you dressed again."

He scoots the chair back then stands up with me still cradled in his arms. I wait for him to set me down. When he doesn't immediately, I get the notion that he isn't going to. Like I said, I'm not that much into public displays of affection, and this counts as one of them.

"Apollo, what are you doing?" I ask, horrified that he's going to carry me out of the room, in front of everyone.

"I'm taking you to the stairs, where I'll wait for you to come down," he responds loudly then looks down at me proudly.

I turn to mush inside. The twins, Jen and Barbie, tall women with my father's dark skin and eyes, crinkle up their mother's small nose and high cheekbones and release duplicate ahhh's behind me. I cringe. Uncle Tommy makes a gagging sign, which tickles the hell out of Derek, of course. My first instinct is to struggle. I can still walk, even if I have to let him do things for me sometimes just to make him happy. And then, I let him have his way just to make him happy.

He crosses the great room, still looking down at me. I'm secretly loving being this close to him and having his undivided attention. By the time he places me on my feet at the bottom of the staircase, I don't want to leave his arms or his presence. So I stand, soaking up his nearness while eye level with his intense gaze. Then he smiles and pats me on the ass.

"Go or I'll kiss you right here, and we know where that will lead, not to talking. And we need to talk, sweetheart."

I nod, then turn, hurrying up the stairs. Every time I look back, he's standing at the bottom like he promised. I realize I'm afraid that he won't be and that he's spoiling me. How will I be able to let him go when it's time for him to fly home?

I don't think I'm going to be able to do it without shedding at least a few tears, at least, not before my independence streak kicks in.

God, I hope it kicks in quickly or I'll shed more than a few.

At the top of the stairs, I turn left toward my parents' room and cover the few steps between the doorway and king-sized bed with thin, curved posts and thick comforter that my father probably kicks on the floor every night. At the edge of the bed, lays the deep-pink ski suit and white fur-lined matching hat and boots, with the tags still on them. I pick it all up and rush back into the hall, peeking over the railing at Apollo, who's still standing at the bottom of the stairs.

I smile then turn down around the corner, to rummage in the boxes for a white T-shirt before closing myself off in my room. I undress and redress in the snug bubble bottoms and matching coat.

Too anxious to be alone with Apollo, I don't bother to put away my first outfit. I want to arrive in record time at the top of the stairs, where I find Apollo is missing.

A cloud of disappointment descends before I take my first step down with the folder in my hand. I set off a loud creak from the aged boards beneath my boot. Apollo appears at the bottom of the stairs immediately, with his coat on, the reason for his disappearance. A stupid grin encompasses my face.

Yep, I'm spoiled now… and I like it.

I pick up the pace in my descent. Apollo grins, and I have to push back the impulse to run to him. When I reach the last step, he just stands, watching me watch him.

"You look like a ski bunny," he says suddenly. "Let me take you to Aspen while we're here."

That trip would be interesting.

"I can't ski, Apollo."

His mouth falls open. "You lived in Colorado, and you can't ski?"

"Living here doesn't make everyone a skier. I didn't want to learn. Looking at the mountains is good enough for me. When did you have time to learn anyway? You were born in an Armani business suit with a contract in both of your hands."

He smirks, which is just as beautiful an expression as any other he wears. "I *was* teenager once, my Lisa, and knew how to have a good time. I want to have one with you. But first, let's go talk, and then I'll teach you. Are we taking your Jeep, my truck, or walking?"

I hope his version of talking is the same as mine.

"Walking," I say before reaching for his hand. "We're just going to the backyard into my father's shed like my mother predicted. We'll still be cold, but we'll be out of the elements."

He opens the front door, steps to the side, and motions with his empty hand for me to take the lead. At the bottom of the front steps, I walk across the front lawn in front of the driveway, to the side of the house, where carefully laid octagon-shaped, concrete blocks begin. They circle around the house to the backyard. An intersecting footpath leads to my father's shed, which is a thousand feet away and is actually a barn that contains his lawn equipment and remnants of his hobbies that he starts but never finishes.

The double doors are unlocked. Apollo reaches around me and pulls one open. A breeze, much colder and sharper than the air outside, slaps me in the face when I walk inside. I veer to the left, to find the light switch and avoid running into the back of the covered old-model car that used to belong to my father's father. It should've been on the road years ago, and I don't think it ever will make it if my father hasn't finished restoring it by now.

Lights flicker on overhead, one at a time, pushing the shadows to the back corners of the barn. I stop beside the hood of the car, letting my eyes roam along the rows of tools mounted on the walls. My mind wanders back in time, to the memories of playing in here with Blake, with and without my father's permission. But I didn't come in here to reminiscence. If I have my way, I'll be making new memories with Apollo, who's standing with his back to the closed doors, watching me closely.

But first things first.

"What did you want to talk about, Apollo?"

"You go first, love. My subject is going to piss you off and you may not even want to be with me after I bring it up."

"Okay." I extend the folder to him, wanting to intrigued by his news. "This is yours. I apologize for Blake's behavior. Yes, I get he was looking into you because of me, but he had no right to dig that far back into your past and I won't lie and say I don't want to know what's in the folder. I also need to apologize for Derek's and my mother's actions. She's been setting you up from the start and pulled Derek into it, who called you a jackass just to see how you'd react at her instigation."

He takes it and flips through the pages. "Yeah, I caught the wink he gave you afterwards. No one calms down that quickly. So they want to know if I'm abusive or psycho. Hopefully, I passed that test, and you're not the only one that wants to see what's in this file."

There's only four pages, but he seems to forget that I'm here with him while reading. Suddenly, he covers his mouth, closes the folder, and lays it on top of the car. I walk to him and wrap my arms around his waist, unable to tell if he's upset or just shocked.

"It's alright, Apollo. I'm here, baby."

His arms encircle my body and pull me even closer. "There's nothing bad in it, sweetheart. At least, nothing bad about my parents except my father has passed. The owners of the orphanage and social workers in Montreal is another matter." He takes a shuddering breath.

I hug him harder, waiting for him to find the words.

"I should probably start at the beginning. Jobs were scarce in the seventies in Montreal. My parents were broke and couldn't afford to take care of me. They trusted the people at the orphanage to do it, while they migrated to the United States with every intention of coming back for me. They did a month later, but the owners of the orphanage had already dumped all the small kids in the system without warning. Apparently, that was routine, just to get a kickback from the mayor for providing the city with a way to get extra money from the government for the Department of Children Services. Most of it went in the corrupt officials' pockets. The foster families got what was left for the kids who all got lost in the system after they changed our last names. Since we were declared as legally abandoned, they could do what they wanted with us and no one could legally give Sienna and Lazarus Ford information on what home I was in. They covered their tracks well. The money kept rolling. I lost the chance to grow up with my parents and my name."

"Does it say where they are?" I ask quietly over my heart breaking for him. He'd lost even more than he thought.

He drops his chin on the top of my head. "My mother is in Newport, Vermont. My father died five years ago. He had a heart attack after they petitioned the government for the tenth time for my last whereabouts. They're still broke, spent every penny they could save on lawyers that are always blocked by the Montreal government. Unless the laws change, she will never know where I am."

"When are you going to see her?"

"As soon as I can, but I need to see about my best girl first."

I smile and tilt my head, to look up at him. "You're always seeing about me and about to open a door that you can't close back, Apollo, so you should probably tell me what's on your mind first." And I hope he talks quickly.

He clears his throat. "It's about Blake. He doesn't like me much and there's a reason for that, which may make making love with me the last thing that you want to do. You may even decide to quit me *and* your job despite the contract you signed that's good for the next seven months."

Immediately, I think Apollo is jealous of not just Derek's new place in my life but Blake's everlasting one, as well.

Just when I don't need any more doubts about us, or my mother being justified in saying, 'I told you so', after this conversation is over.

"Apollo, your place in my life is solid."

"I'm not jealous of Blake's position in your family, sweetheart, and I hope for your sake that he isn't jealous of mine, or things are about to get awkward... but he doesn't just feel brotherly towards you either."

What?

I step back out of his reach, thoroughly shocked. "That's not true, Apollo. He's just seeking the love that his family wouldn't or couldn't give him as child. He'll grow up soon... I hope."

"That may be true, my Lisa. But Blake still likes you as much more than a surrogate sister. How could he not when you're beautiful and he's intelligent as hell?"

"Apollo, I don't want to argue about this. I'm going back inside the house." I push off the car to walk away, then change my mind. I'm essentially running away from the situation, when this is one that I need to face head on, for Apollo's and my sake, and Blake's. "Why would you even say that, Apollo?"

He stuffs his hands in his pockets. "A grown man doesn't sleep with his sister."

A fierce need to defend my family rises.

"What Blake did last night may seem weird to you, Apollo, but it's not for us. We took him in when his was just a child, even though he wasn't an orphan. He's slept with me, or by my bed, since he was seven. My mother believes he's still looking for his place in this world, and I believe her. I haven't seen or talked to him in years, so maybe he's still looking for this right place for him and sticking close to me while he does it. I can't just push him away if being at my side makes him feel better when I'm around."

"I get that, my Lisa. But why your *bedside*? Why would he just go all incommunicado if he still needs you to find his place, and then jump back in your bed as soon as you show up at home? If he doesn't want you, then he sure as hell doesn't want you with me."

I grow cold all over.

"Are you saying he's a deal breaker? Are we destined to break up only after a few hours in each other's company every single time a problem pops up? That's not fair... at least not to me, Apollo. I didn't encourage Blake to pick my lock and crawl into bed with me last night, especially after he stuck me on the no-fly list just to keep me here because he's worried about me concerning you. He does crazy shit like that, but you wouldn't know that because you don't know him."

Apollo walks up to me. "He doesn't know you anymore either, my Lisa, and vice versa. Eight years is a long time to be apart from someone. What worries me the most is that he didn't concern himself with what you'd want when he crawled into bed with you. If that doesn't worry you, it sure as hell worries me."

"Family doesn't concern themselves with your feelings when they're worried about you, Apollo. The proof of that is in the folder laying on top of the car."

"Maybe they should concern themselves. Not doing that sometimes makes whatever you're going through worse. I don't have to have a family to know that."

Oh, things have certainly gotten worse.

I point toward the house, while doing my best not to get extremely angry with Apollo. "Tell that to my family about making things worse, Apollo. If I had my way, no one would've found out that you'd broken my heart, or about this conversation." I found him twice after losing him once, and I don't want to go through that again. I don't want to go through the last two days again, ever.

"Then don't tell everyone, but I think your mother, out of all of them, will already know what I'm telling you. Not much gets past her."

I shiver with dread. Apollo has to be completely convinced of Blake's feelings for me if he thinks my mother can corroborate what he believes when he can't be sure if she approves of him this early in our relationship. This means I need to face what he believes about Blake, even if I don't want to... ever. I owe it to Apollo *and* Blake to get to the bottom of this and set Blake straight if his heart has a place in it for me that he doesn't have in mine.

"Trust me, Apollo. I know doesn't much get past her. I'm just surprised that you want me to take this to her, and eventually to him."

"Sweetheart, that's because I know I'm right. When there's something you need to know, I'm going to tell you, whether you want to hear it or not. Yes, I know this conversation is uncomfortable for you and makes me look even more jealous than I've already been pegged to be. It may even make me look like a mad man who's trying to cause a rift in your family. But I'm going to speak the truth, and I'll deal with the fallout... whatever that may be."

At this point, I can't beat Apollo's conviction with a stick, not when most people are rather fond of lying and keeping things hidden. He's pushing for out in the open. I just wish he wasn't pushing it in my direction.

"You're willing to lose me just to tell me truth?"

"Yes," he says sincerely, with a stream of regret rolling in his eyes.

I can clearly see that he hates to be the one to tell me this, so I have to believe him, at least about what he *thinks* is true. He's willing to risk it all to open my eyes, even if I prefer to leave them wide shut when it comes to Blake. This is something I just don't want to see or believe.

If I do, it changes everything that I want to stay the same. Blake, along with the rest of my family, is a constant in my life. A comforting one, whether we keep in touch or not. If Blake has feelings for me, this changes everything. Things would be easier if I had proof that Blake's affections rose above stepbrother, but I don't, and neither does Apollo.

I'm dealing with a whole bunch of 'ifs' here that may ruin my family. I can't exactly see myself walking up to Blake and asking him to check a yes or no box on a letter, like a fifth grader. I sure as hell wouldn't ask him about his feelings for me out loud for the family to overhear or in a digital form that can be shared. Some things need to be kept just between two people and their significant others, except Blake doesn't have one. Or does he?

"Apollo, Blake's never said or done anything out of the way toward me romantically."

Neither did Apollo, Malisa, and look how well that turned out. If you don't see this through, you really don't trust Apollo like you should, especially not with your heart.

"Neither did—"

I raise my hand, cutting him off. "Yeah, yeah, Apollo, neither did you. I'm way ahead of you. God, I just don't need this right now. Not with me trying to find my place in your life."

I'm still sure that we shouldn't be working together though. We're still not going to get any work done when I feel free to get in his pants.

Apollo's hands rocket out of his pockets and land on my arms. "Your place with me is one damn thing you never have to worry about. It's yours. Your name is stamped on it, me, and whatever else I have. But I'm sure Blake will tell you the truth, whatever that may be. And I know for a fact that he'll find you if I find some other place else to be, which will be the right time to ask him."

Don't leave me, again, I think. Although I know I have to face Blake alone, how can I trust my heart with Apollo if he's always running off?

I should be asking him that.

"Apollo, you're going to—"

"Nowhere," he cuts in then grins. "Learned that lesson already. I don't have to leave your family's home to give you space with your family. I've been offered the guest bedroom across the hall from you and I'm taking it." He pulls me into his arms and holds me so tightly I can barely breathe, as if he's trying to make our bodies into one, and it's what I need.

How he knows that, I have no idea, but it sure as hell imbeds him deeper in my heart, and a little more of it steps over the line to his side, along with my trust. I don't know many people who'll detonate a bomb in the middle of someone's world, then stick around to watch it blow up.

I swing my arms around his waist, bury my head in his chest, and hold on for dear life. The foundation of my world is cracking, and he's all that's holding it and me together, right now.

"Tell me how long you need me to hold you, my Lisa, and I will."

"Forever and a day," I whisper.

"You got it, babe." A soft a kiss is planted on the crown of my head then Apollo's breath traipses across my ear. "Whatever you need, you got it," he whispers, inciting sharp pangs of desire in my core.

I tilt my head back, my chin in his chest.

"You know what I need, Apollo."

He looks down at me and smiles even harder. "I think I can help with that."

"Can you?"

"Damn straight. Walk with me."

"Walk? What I want, you can't do while walking."

"That's what you think, but you're not going to get what you want today, just a mild version of it, and quickly."

"Well, that's cryptic."

"But I keep my word."

"True, but—"

"Walk, my Lisa."

"This had better be good," I gripe then step back.

"It will be. Trust me." Apollo snags my hand in his and moves past me, toward the front end of the car.

I follow because it's time that I did trust him completely. At least I'll be all in, and I'll sleep at night knowing I'd given my all and tried my best to make us work. He is my world and I firmly believe that I'm his, finally.

Chapter Seventeen

"I just wish I didn't have to face Blake alone," I grumble under my breath. "He'll probably pinch me. He used to do that all the time when we were little."

Apollo howls with laughter, while going deeper into the shed, then he glances back. "I'll sit by your side while you talk with him, if you go with me to meet my mother. I'm not giving her a warning that I'm coming either, because I want to know why I was dropped off an orphanage with no warning. Fair is fair as far as I'm concerned. Only God knows how that meeting's going to turn out."

"It's probably best if I talk with Blake alone. Who wants to have their heart broken with an audience? But I'm praying you're wrong about Blake, and yes, I'll go with you to meet your mother. No one should do something like that alone."

Apollo stops in his tracks and looks down at me with a pensive gaze and a small smile playing across his face. "You'd do that for me?"

"Of course, I would. That'll be much easier than talking to Blake by myself. You offered to do it with me, so I have to show my appreciation for your willingness to face that music somehow."

"In that case, I think I can give you what you want."

"What I want, huh?"

"Yes… and quickly. Someone is going to have a reason to come out here in about fifteen minutes."

"I warned you," I quip.

"You did, but I had no idea how special you really are to your family, or how nosy they are."

I'm laughing my ass off and loudly when Apollo stops in front of an old workbench of my father's. It's positioned at the very back of the barn where there's less light and more privacy. The dust that's settled on the flat surface of the bench is thick enough to choke a human to death. Apollo drops my hand to shrug out of his coat.

"What are you doing?" I ask, while eyeing the work bench warily.

It'll hold my weight, but Apollo's coat will be ruined if he lays it on top of it.

"I'm doing what you think I'm doing, and you should be unzipping your coat and pants if you want what I plan to give you."

I look at him suspiciously next. "Which is?"

"My mouth… on you… in here… right now. Take it or leave it."

His devilish grin comes out to play before he swivels at the waist to spread his coat along the wide board nailed to the top of the work bench. I lift an eyebrow, wary of sitting anywhere near the work bench, let alone on it. Then I reach for the zipper of my coat. I'd risk anything to be with this man.

My nipples are already pebbled and pushing against my shirt before the icy air can touch them through the thin material of my T-shirt. Apollo reaches for the zipper of my jeans. The teeth grinding open is enough to set my nerves on edge and my insides on fire. Undoing my zipper with his eyes on me just makes the inferno within me worse. I welcome the frigid air playing around my warm thighs, as I push down my pants and underwear below them.

"That's far enough, my Lisa. I don't want you to catch hypothermia."

My hands freeze in place. His hands glide underneath my arms and lift me off my feet. He sets me gently down on top of his coat. I brace my weight on my hands then lean back on the bench. Apollo runs his hands up my abdomen to knead my breasts, sending bursts of pleasure from one end of me to the other. Then he bends at the waist and bites my nipples through my outer layers of clothing.

156

His warm breath breaches my shirt and violates the flesh beneath it, before tickling the rim of my senses. The room curls around the edges. I start to rock on the bench, equilibrium thrown completely off.

"Apollo, I'm dizzy, and I won't be able to sit up much longer. Get to the good part, already."

He chuckles into my chest quietly then drops to his knees on the cold, concrete floor that's speckled with oil spots and dirt. His hands wrap around my ankles in the thick boots.

"Bend and spread your knees, sweetheart."

I do. He ducks, and then his head appears between my legs. Suddenly, he's eye to eye with my honeypot. The sight alone is erotic enough to make me groan and my head too heavy to hold up. It drops back on my shoulders, while heat blasts through me. The force of it makes me sway side to side on the bench. I'm lightheaded from just imagining what he's going to do to me.

My legs, still trapped in the confines of my pants, drop down on his shoulders. Then Apollo's mouth is kissing the lips between my thighs. He begins to suckle at my clitoris, and all my common sense goes out the window, allowing massive amounts of bliss in sharp and dull forms to come in and undulate through my core.

It's all too much to withstand, and I need relief in the first seconds of having his mouth on me. I squeal, then try to fold up on myself. My pants pull on the nape of his neck, drawing his head deeper into the vee of my thighs, giving him even more access to my body.

His tongue glides between the wet rims of my southbound mouth and knock at the door of my body, before the tip of his tongue enters, crooks, and laps at the roof of my tunnel. More knife-like ripples and dull machete swipes collide with the soft tissue in my canal. A sleeping giant unfurls in my core and stretches out, reaching up into my abdomen and deep into the tunnel filled with his tongue. The waking orgasm sinks its claws deep into me and pulls its way to full alertness, dulling my senses and sharpening them at the same time, until I can't make heads or tails of anything.

When it takes me completely over, pressure discharges in the places where the waking orgasm has me gripped tightly. I start to pant, fighting for every breath I take. It almost hurts to cum on Apollo's face, but I endure the force spiraling through me by praying for it to stop soon. His tongue begins to rocket in and out of me, interrupting the monster waves coursing through me.

They rebound, fighting for all the space inside me. More pressure spreads out through me and pounds me from the inside out, angrily. One body can only tolerate so much heaven being forced on it, and I'm well past my limit. When the waves taper off, I inhale the cold air in the barn, welcoming it into my starving lungs.

"Please, Apollo, stop." I have no shame about begging if it gets me what I want—relief from my release.

He hums against my flesh, and ticks off the fading monster orgasm. It picks up in intensity, again.

I scream, "No more, Apollo!"

"You sure, sweetheart?" he asks, and I've never been so glad for his mouth to be talking instead of kissing my body.

"Yes," I hiss, then drop down on my elbows, unable to hold my upper torso up any longer.

"Then you're ready for *me* then."

I shake my head. I've had all I can take of him.

He grins. "Oh yes, you're ready, love. You said you wanted it on the front porch, and now you're going to get it."

I gasp at the most sensual threat that I've ever heard. But anymore of him inside me will wipe me out completely. Except, I can't bring myself to make him aware of this, and I don't want to.

He stands up, pushing my pants and underwear further down my legs. They stop at the tops of my boots, trapping Apollo inside them with me, my legs around his waist. He spreads the opened ends of his jeans further apart. The enormous lump of his manhood resting at his waist twitches inside his gray briefs, and distracts me from the uncomfortable nips of his zipper. His erection is as much a prisoner in Apollo's underwear as he is in mine.

My tunnel spasms, contracting and releasing greedily for more of Apollo, even as I'm spent. He pushes at the waistline of his briefs, until his stiff rod plops out. He palms it, positions it at my entrance, and shoves into me until he bottoms out. His penetration is much deeper than I anticipated, pushing past the very center of me.

Pain and pleasure fire off my overly sensitive nerve endings. I rocket up to a sitting position, hoping to lessen his possession and staunch the flow of sensations, while gasping for air and grasping for him with both hands. They grab the shirt at his chest then make tight fists in it. I look up, pleading with him silently to change his mind about making love to me.

He shakes his head then leans forward, forcing me right back to where I started. Except, I'm flat on my back against the workbench instead of on my elbows, completely exposed to whatever he decides to do me. His hands grip my hips, and he withdraws from my body, only to sink even deeper into me. Then he freezes in place, leaving me on overly full. He should be able to feel my lungs seizing.

"Fuck, Malisa!" he hisses through his clenched teeth.

I hiss right back, "You got that damn right, Apollo! I can feel you in my damn chest."

"Then I'm about to fuck the shit out of your lungs, sweetheart." And I believe him.

"God no," I whisper.

"He can't save you now, sweetheart. You're too damn tight and wet, and I'm resisting the urge to slam into you and break your back as it is, because that's all I want to do right now."

"Jesus, Apollo. How long will it take you to cum?" I've passed the limit of how much I can take now.

"However long it takes me, my Lisa," he says arrogantly, and then reverses until only the tip of him is teasing the wet folds of my body.

When he moves, the bench rocks backward with his movement, threatening to pitch me on the floor head first.

"Apollo!" I yell, and grip his shirt even tighter.

He pulls my hips toward him, forcing the backs of my thighs to meet his jeans-clad ones in the backbreaking collisions he promised, while resetting the bench without breaking his pace.

"I got you, love. Always."

I believe that, too. But I'd rather have my feet planted firmly on the floor, except that's just not going to happen until Apollo has done what he's set his mind to, cumming inside me. He starts with conquering pleasure zones and stroking white hot places within me, then detonating grenades of pure ecstasy in each place, until it feels like claws are sinking into my tunnel and abdomen again.

"No, no, no," I murmur, knowing what I'm in for.

I most certainly don't want to cum, again.

The home that he's made inside my body collapses around the base of his shaft, hoping to stop all movement. Apollo forces his way out of the trap that my flesh failed to set, and then he forces his way back inside it.

"Fuck yes, Malisa," he groans above me. "Keep milking my cock like that and this will be over much faster than you think."

My tunnel begins to contract and release on its own around him, hoping to push him over the edge. If I keep this up, I'm going to throw myself right over it with him. Moisture seeps out of my body, coating my thighs. Apollo's pace rises from backbreaking to breakneck.

"Fuck, Apollo!" I yell out. "I'm going to cum."

"Me too, love. Cum with me."

I begin to tumble in a groundless sky at his command. He shoves up into me, piercing my womb, and then collapses on top of me, burying his head in my neck and growling in my ear. A scrap of pain imbeds itself in the pleasure surging through me and raises the strength of my climax up a notch. I wrap my arms around his neck tightly and wait for the hell raining down inside me to die down.

Apollo's chest heaves against mine that's rising and sinking in sync with his. We lay this way, with me praying that the bench holds up until we're both breathing normally again and can get up. His head lifts and he gives me a soft kiss on the mouth. I part my lips. His tongue slips inside and takes slow sideswipes at mine until I shiver.

"Cold, love?"

I nod. He gives me a loud smack on the mouth, making me giggle, and then he stands up within the confines of my ski pants.

"Let's go, my Lisa, before someone shows up and realizes that I'm dirty and you're not, and then I become the butt of one of your uncle Tommy's jokes. We've been gone…" He looks down at the Cartier watch on his wrist. "…for thirty minutes."

I push up on my elbows. "Hell, I'm surprised we got ten."

Apollo drops to his knees and wiggles his way out of my pants. "Maybe your mother feels like I'm good for you now. At least I hope she does anyway, because I'm not going anywhere."

"She's certainly the main one to worry about," I grumble, while he stands up, slips his hand under my arms, and stands me up on my feet before fastening up his pants.

I start to do the same, but it's a slow process. I'm exhausted, and all I want to do is sleep, and I intend to.

"What are we going to do next, sweetheart?" he asks, while reaching behind me for his coat, with layers of dust entrenched in the silky material.

He knocks off as much as he can, but the last layer of dust refuses to budge. He gives up and puts his coat on.

I bend over and swipe at the dirt sticking to the knees of his pants. "I'm going back to bed, Apollo, as soon as I get in the house. You wore me out."

He snickers low in his throat. "Your family will know what we've been doing out here if you go straight to sleep."

"That will be kind of a dead giveaway, huh?" I giggle.

"You think?" he joins my laughter. "I intended to wear you out, so you don't gorge yourself on me while we're here. Obviously, I can't resist you when you want me."

"Four years can't be made up for in one night, Apollo," I say softly.

"True, but I have the feeling you'd try to do it anyway."

"Damn straight."

"You are always a determined little minx. It's what I love about you the most."

"That comes with the independent streak."

"The good with the bad, huh?" He pulls me into his arms and pecks me on the nose. "I can deal with it, love, if you can."

"I plan to, Apollo."

"And I love you for it, my Lisa."

"God, I missed your version of my name."

"You made me afraid to even call you by it on the phone yesterday."

"I thought it was best if we went back to employee and employer."

"Not as long as I love you, and I plan to love you until the next lifetime, where I'll find you again."

"I love you, too Apollo. Always have."

"Then love me enough to get me out of this cold ass barn. When I'm not inside you, I'd like to be wherever the heat is."

"So, my guy is cold-natured, huh?" No wonder he wears full suits even in the summertime.

"Very. Besides, I also need to check on some things, and your mother offered me her landline."

I smile, then turn away, keeping one of his hands gripped tightly in mine, while leading him back to the house, where the heat is plentiful.

At the front door, he spins me around to face him. He's suddenly serious. "If you need help with Blake, just yell, and I'll come running. I promise."

Suddenly, I'm not so tired anymore, but conflicted. "Blake won't hurt me. I just hope I don't hurt him. I think I'll take a shower and wait to catch him alone. I don't want this going on one more day."

"You can't make him turn his feelings off."

"I don't think his feelings are that deep for me. But I need to talk to him to know for sure, so we all can move on. I have the man I want, need, and I intend to keep him. I haven't even started making up for the time we lost yet, and I never will if you keep fucking my brains out before I can get *my* hands and mouth on your body."

"You're time will come to handle me as you see fit, but you should probably just mark the time we circled each other as a lesson learned then move on." He leans closer, lining his lips with mine. "Because I love fucking your brains out as much I love you."

He lips gently trace mine before his tongue parts the seam of my lips. They open up automatically to let him inside. The front door opens behinds us. Apollo's tongue slips from my mouth. He looks up then down at me. I know instantly who's standing behind me.

He pats me on the ass then steps back. "Go shower, love. Come find me when you're done spending time with the family."

I nod and swallow deeply, then let my hands drift off his waist before I turn around to face Blake. He's eating a slice of bacon and looking down at me with blank blue eyes. It's not like Blake to hide his feelings from me. I begin to wonder how long he has been doing it.

No time like the present to find out.

"Blake, can you meet me outside in thirty minutes? I need to talk to you."

His stare hardens then drifts upward to Apollo. The air gets crisp around us and heavy with tension.

"Sure, Malisa. Thirty minutes it is." He swivels in the doorway then vanishes into the kitchen.

Apollo glances down at me. "I'll be just up the stairs, sweetheart. If you need me, just holler."

"Blake won't hurt me, love."

"I don't care if he just pinches you, holler. Got it?"

I start to laugh, even with the gloom and doom that's surrounding us. "Got it."

Chapter Eighteen

A knock at my bedroom door comes just as I tug on the second wedge heel boot on top of my jeans that I'd exchanged for the ski suit. My shower had woken me up a little more, but the heavy atmosphere is still around, waiting to combust.

"Come in," I yell from my seat on the bed.

The door opens. Blake steps inside, empty-handed.

"Shut it back, Blake, while I put on my coat, or someone will see us in here and interrupt before we can get downstairs."

"Oh, this has to be bad. Apollo managed to turn you against me that quick?" He shuts the door back then props against the wall and crosses his arms. "So talk, Malisa."

"Apollo didn't turn anybody, Blake. But there's something bugging the hell out of us both." I reach for my coat lying beside me.

"Finding me in bed with you will bug the man who loves you like he does."

I turn around and shove my arms inside the ski jacket. "He thinks you're at least attracted to me, and he understands because he's crazy enough to think I'm beautiful… and irresistible, I guess. But I'm having a hard time agreeing with him."

"What do you think?" he asks, immediately alerting me to the fact that he didn't adamantly deny his attraction.

"I… don't… well, I think you're like a brother to me," I stammer to admit.

"Well, Apollo is the one who got it right," Blake says as his eyes burrow into me. "After all this time, it took him to pick up on my secret. I tried to hide it all these years, so no one, not even Mama O and Pop, would sniff out my attraction to you. I've even tried to fight it, but it just won't go away, so I managed it through self-control."

Shock paralyzes me.

"Shit," I mumble under my breath, "It's true."

Blake nods, with regret sitting deep in his eyes. I start to fidget under his gaze, and then I shift on the bed, trying to find a comfortable place in a usually comfortable bed. But it's just not possible with this conversation.

"It is true, Lisa Poo. You're beautiful, even freaking more so now without the ponytails and glasses, which is probably driving Apollo to drink, and why I preferred the less erotic version of you. But I haven't been waiting for you to come back to Colorado so we could fall in love, if that's what he's thinking."

"Well, yeah, I know you haven't been waiting for me because we haven't seen each other since you left Arrow. Now I'm wondering why we haven't talked? And why I don't know you like I used to or thought I did."

"Nobody knows anyone like they think they do unless they're married. I left Arrow because I needed some distance from my parents' after the 'becoming a true Powers argument'. I'm not into social gatherings and charity events, and I needed some distance for two reasons. To figure out my own path in life and to let my attraction to you die down. Talking to you and visiting you wouldn't have done that. We can rectify the distance between us by you telling me what did Apollo do that had you running back home with a broken heart. I haven't exactly given my heart away to anyone," he admits.

"Why not?" I ask, beginning to worry as much about him as my mother does.

He deserves to be loved just like everyone else does, but he doesn't seem to be reaching out for it beyond the Owens clan.

His head drifts downward and he begins to pick at imaginary lint on his sweater. "Because my family is pressing me to move back home and be a true Powers, or so that's what they're calling it. I've never felt like a Powers, and can't date anyone with that shit hanging over my head. You would think my father's stroke would've given my parents a clearer insight into what matters the most, but it hasn't."

Blake truly hasn't found his place in this world because he has too many places to choose from.

"Is it because you feel like an Owens through and through that you're stuck? If so, it's your parents' fault that you feel closer to us, Blake, not yours." And he should stop beating himself up about it.

"I'm an Owens, Malisa, and I know that it's my parents' fault, but it's also why I never let my school boy crush on you get any further than that. It would feel sort of like incest for one thing, and if things went bad between us, Mama O and Pop would have to choose. I'm not taking the chance of getting pushed out of this family. It's the only good one I've known. I'm not losing it because I can recognize a beautiful woman when I see one either, and I'm still twisted inside with which family to be the most loyal to. Being a true Powers would take up all my time."

"Lydia and Frank wouldn't choose between us, Blake, or make you choose which family to be loyal to. They'd be disappointed in us if we couldn't work things out like adults, even if a romantic relationship didn't work out between us. The Owens will stand by whatever decision you make about becoming a true Powers... whatever that means. No need to be twisted inside. Just make a decision that will make you happy and then move on. And Blake... if it's just a school boy crush and you still own your heart, then we're fine."

"You're damn straight we're fine, Lisa Poo. There's no way in hell I'd let anything come in between me and the people that loved me when my own parents wouldn't. And I'm sticking around to make sure Apollo does right by you, no matter what feelings about you war inside of me. You're still my sister."

Thank God!

The tension eases away finally.

I smile at him with my stupid eyes burning. "Always."

"Good. Now go get me some blankets, so I can sleep beside your bed on the floor tonight. I'm sure finding me *in* it is what gave me away to Apollo this morning, and I may have silently challenged him. I don't want to come in between your happiness, either, but I'm certainly taking the chance to make him sweat tonight."

Nothing has changed with Blake, at all.

I start to laugh. "You don't stop, do you?"

He smiles wide. "I would, but I have nowhere else to sleep. I'm not going home while you're here. We need to get to know one another, again. Uncle Tommy is staying for the night in my room. Apollo's in the guestroom. Oh, and Derek told me to tell you goodbye but he'll be back tomorrow. He still has to work and the temperature's dropping as we speak, even though it's only twelve in the afternoon. I think a freak storm is coming in. Derek's Cessna is an older model. Its wings aren't equipped to handle the ice that'll form on them when he's flying, which will bring him down like a rock in a swimming pool. I should tell you that he's interested in Chrys and through working for Mama O because she fired him after you and Apollo left the dining room. I think Chrys is interested in him as well because she offered to take him to the airport."

"Good for them."

His forehead wrinkles. "You don't mind?"

"Why would I? Derek and I never dated. We'd already decided to be friends before he even flew here, and Apollo cut him off at the knees Saturday night."

Blake smirks then his chest begins to rumble with his rising mirth. "Apollo isn't someone I would want to go against during a war. He'd find my weakest spot before I could."

"It's funny you said that, Blake, because I feel the same damn way about him. He sees a lot and is sneaky as hell."

"I'll bet. I'm sure he snuck his way into your heart, too."

168

"From the damn moment I laid eyes on him. I couldn't even speak, and the damn fool hired me anyway."

"That's because he's smart as hell, knows a good thing when he sees it and how to keep it close. I could maybe learn a few things from him."

I cock an eyebrow. "*Maybe*, Blake?"

"I said maybe. Now back to your love life." He pushes off the wall and palms the doorknob before opening it. "Let's go inside."

I stand up and follow him out. "One session of my love life isn't going to cover the four years we've been out of touch, Dr. Phil," I quip.

He smirks, the usual boyish appeal returning to his face. "You'd be amazed at what Dr. Phil can do in one session."

"You're right about that, but you're not him," I admit while walking down the stairs.

"No, I'm Sheriff Powers and much better. So, can I tell you what I think happened between you and your boss?"

"Shoot, Sheriff Powers… or not."

Oddly, it feels good to talk to someone that's known me longer than a few days, and it doesn't feel weird that it's Blake, even if he is attracted to me in some way. I could always tell him anything; he's family.

Blake reaches the front door then glances back, before opening it.

"Funny, Lisa Poo. Your first cop joke at my expense, and it failed epically, by the way. Over the weekend, Apollo screwed up. It had to be real bad for you to come home, because it's not like you to run from anything. He got back to Utah before you did and was expecting your return, or at least a call since Sunday. When he didn't get it, he called here that evening, and was panicking like a lover would, and it got worse with each call. I think it's safe to assume that's he's been a lover of yours at least since Saturday, because employers

169

don't follow behind their employees unless there's an emotional bond… or was. Am I right?"

"Yes," I say simply, and close the front door behind me.

Blake takes the first step down off the porch. "That's why I risked pissing you off to invite Apollo here. I needed him on my territory. Did you really think I wanted to just get to know your boss?"

"No, I guess not. Not when it comes to this family." And that's what Blake and I will always be, but Apollo seems to be getting all the blame for our break up in Blake's eyes.

I accept that I need to reveal the details of our split before Apollo is condemned in everyone's opinions. "To be honest, Blake, I unintentionally started the problem between me and Apollo by raising hell about him paying for everything during my trip without asking me. It happened while I was out shopping. I thought I'd get the chance to make up with him, but he sent a taxi driver to take me back to the hotel, which he'd already fled from like an escapee. The driver gave me a message to return to work Tuesday morning, when he and I was supposed to go back together. But he left me in Vegas, after he wasn't supposed to be there in the first place."

Blake stops walking when he reaches the back of my Jeep. I take a seat on the frozen rear bumper, with him standing in front of me. He pushes the tips of his fingers into his jeans pockets, as if they're cold, and they should be in this weather. Even with the sun blazing down on us, its heat isn't reaching beyond the scattered clouds floating lazily in the sky.

Blake cocks his head to the side. "What do you mean he wasn't supposed to be in Vegas?"

"We didn't decide to become a couple until Saturday night. I left Friday on vacation, with every intention of leaving my crush on Apollo at work with him. He followed me to profess his love for me, then confessed on Sunday that he'd paid for everything; my room, plane ticket, makeover, and he wanted to pay for the wardrobe that I'd left him in bed to go shop for. When I told him no he couldn't fund my shopping spree, that I was independent, he got pissed. But, it was a beautiful and quiet furious. And then I said I could carry my own bags. He told me he'd get out of my way and let me do everything for myself, since that's what I wanted. Then he flew away. When I got the message from the taxi driver that I shouldn't come back to work 'til Tuesday morning, nothing can explain how depressed I felt." Abandoned even.

"You thought he didn't want you around until then, and the relationship was over before it ever saw the light of day."

I nod. Blake starts to laugh his ass off loudly. I'm not surprised, because I knew he'd find my heartache funny, just not this damn funny.

"Malisa, you don't know much about men, do you?"

I scoff, "I guess not. But you're going to tell me what I don't know, aren't you?"

"Oh yeah, but inside. I'm cold." He unearths one hand to reach for mine.

I hesitate to take his fingers reddened at the fingertips, for just plain and simple get back.

"Please, Lisa Poo! I won't put you on the no-fly list again," he whines, suddenly pissy.

I giggle and take his hand, which swallows mine. "Quit crying, Blake, and leave some for the baby. Who in the hell gave you that kind of power anyway, Sheriff Powers?"

"The city of Arrow, like damn fools, after my parents threatened to stop donating to its various fundraisers." he admits. "At least they're good for a cushy job." Then he laughs before stiffening, as if someone dropped an ice cube down his sweater.

"Lisa Poo, are you…" his voice fades.

I understand, immediately, where his mind had gone. "God no, I'm not pregnant." But Apollo and I hadn't used protection either time we were together. "At least, I don't think..." And then, my words quit coming altogether.

I know a few moments of superb sex can have far-reaching consequences. At least, that's what the Sex Ed teacher, Mrs. Scion, preached in middle school. Apparently, I wasn't listening when she said protect yourself.

Blake tugs on my hand. "Inside, Malisa. We'll finish this in the kitchen, and I'll start in on your boyfriend tomorrow."

I tug back. "Don't say anything to anyone about this."

"As much as you like to believe that you can handle anything alone, Malisa, you can't. Not this, anyway."

"Blake, I don't know if I am pregnant. It's too early to tell, and Apollo should know before everyone else."

The front door opens suddenly. I peer up at Blake, pleadingly. He nods, reluctantly. He'll hate keeping my parents in the dark, but he has to respect my wishes. It's my secret. Maybe, there isn't a baby to keep secret.

Oh God, I hope not. Apollo and I can barely keep us together.

My mother steps out onto the porch, hugging herself. "Everything okay? You two have been out for a few minutes and it's too cold for even that." Blake and I start toward her.

He looks up at my mother. "Nothing to be worried about, Mama O. Well... nothing life doesn't throw everybody's way eventually."

She sniffs. "So, it was love then?"

Blake nods.

Oh my damn, they'd been discussing me behind my back anyway.

She grins. "Told you that you're nothing but a worrywart, Blake. Malisa, do you know he planned to take your poor boss to the woods and pull his gun on him, just to make Apollo tell what he'd done to you?"

I stop in my tracks. Blake gets tugged backwards before he knows to stop. Then he looks back at me, grinning.

"You didn't?" I ask, but I don't know why I bothered.

This is right up Blake's alley.

He grins roguishly. "I did and I will."

I shake my head and close my eyes. "Blake, you're destined to end up in your own handcuffs."

He tugs on my hand and pulls me toward the steps. "For breaking my sister's heart, I'd do a hell of a lot worse."

"Watch your mouth, Blake," Lydia warns.

"Lisa Poo cussed earlier and you didn't say that to her," he whines, while taking the first stair.

She glares at Blake, with her eyes narrowed. "You'd already ticked her off by putting her on the no-fly list. Of course, I didn't say anything."

Then she turns to me with the same glare, which she's been giving us since I could remember. It's like you're peering into a black abyss that will swallow you whole if you don't give it what it wants. It's still scary as hell, and just makes it easier to give her what she wants.

"So, are you still leaving?" she asks.

If I was, I wouldn't be after that look.

"No, we're staying for a few days."

"Why didn't you just give her the black stare yesterday, Mama O?" Blake asks then exhales heavily, faking frustration. "We could've avoided me putting her on the no-fly list."

"Because you'd forced her behind her bedroom door, *Blake*. If I'd went in, then she'd have just walked around me, got in her Jeep, and left."

Frank walks out behind Lydia. "So Blake got out of Malisa whatever she didn't want to tell us, huh?"

Lydia nods.

My father trains his stare on Blake. "Well… how bad is it? Do we still take Apollo to the woods and actually bury him or just threaten?"

I stare at them slack-jawed. My father was in on Blake's plot to scare the hell out Apollo, and it is going to happen if my father condones it.

"Daddy!" I cry. "What are you two thinking? You can't just drive people to the woods and threaten them."

Blake and Frank share a look of conspirators.

Lydia closes her eyes and shakes her head. "Malisa, they've been doing it since you started dating at sixteen."

I develop the early stages of shock. Every boy I'd been interested in at school would always suddenly become interested in someone else. Even though the girls that picked up my latest crush would become pregnant or the talk of Arrow for one reason or another, I'd started to think I was a leper, until I went off to college and met Mark Davidson. We became good friends and secret lovers until we graduated. I never brought him home to meet my family, and now I know why I had to wait to lose my virginity.

My head swivels between the first male loves of my life. "Did you two do this every time I liked someone?"

"Yep," they chant together, proudly.

Blake chuckles quietly beside me. "We invited them over for a surprise dinner for you behind your back and offered to pick them up from their houses. They got in the car every time, but they never made it here."

"Oh my God!" I shriek. "I thought I was the reason I never had a boyfriend longer than five seconds."

Frank drops a hand on Lydia's shoulder. "If their intentions toward you were pure, you would've had one, baby girl. We gave them all the choice to be a real boyfriend, leave you alone, or visit their final resting place in the woods permanently. They wisely chose to leave you alone, so you could find someone who didn't want to run through you, and they could live to select the next girl on their hit list."

I sigh and mumble, "Most of those girls have an eight-year old or a STD on their medical record. So thanks, guys."

Blake shakes his head hard enough to knock at least one of his senses loose. "What you say, Lisa Poo?"

"I said thank you! Dammit!"

He taps his cheek. "Right here, Lisa Poo."

My parents snigger. I refuse Blake's demand with a swipe of my hand through the air.

"I'm not kissing you for ruining my love life when I was already an ugly duckling." Then I realize my bad choice of words with my mother in the vicinity.

Chapter Nineteen

"Malisa Owens," she starts, "You are not and you never were an ugly anything. I didn't encourage you to get rid of your glasses or let your hair down, which you have done. Now, you brought *two* men to my house. So there, you can blame me too for your stunted… love… life." She turns to my father. "Oh God! Just saying those words makes me cold all over, Frank."

He frowns and pulls her face first into his chest and wraps his arms around her.

"You all just picked up where you left off when I showed up yesterday," I accuse, with a grin.

How did I miss what they were doing all those years? Apollo was in for a bad time if he got in the car with either one of them, and I better warn him before he does.

"Oh, you will not be warning, Apollo," Blake says out of nowhere. "He missed the whole 'if you hurt my sister, this is where you'll lay for eternity' in the woods speech. I aim to fix that, and I'll confiscate your phone on suspicious terrorist activity, convince Mr. Lindsey to say he thinks Apollo broke into his hotel in the pretense of hauling Apollo's ass off to jail, and get him to the woods anyway."

My parents find that extremely funny, my father most of all. "Good one, son. I couldn't have pulled that off as a pediatrician."

I shake my head. "Is there any length you two won't go to?"

"Nope," they chant together.

Blake bursts out laughing. "We haven't had this much fun together in years, Pop."

"No, we haven't son, but Malisa is here now and the games can begin."

Lydia giggles harder into my father's chest. "You two are sick. When she leaves, she probably won't come back."

Frank's mouth drops open. "Oh, you're denying that you're the mastermind behind Blake's and my criminal activities, Lydia. Shame on you."

She flushes a beet red. I turn to her. She shrugs.

"Sorry, baby girl, but you're my only daughter and no one ever hurts you or wants to hurt you and gets away with it. I'd planned to be the leg breaker myself. But Frank and Blake said actual violence wasn't necessary to get my point across."

Frank nods. "So yes, we took her directions and then executed them with finesse, before Lydia got herself locked up."

"You three had better tell me what all you've done and who you did it to," I demand. "For all I know, there's a bunch of dead bodies in the woods and I'll have to use Apollo's clout to keep you *all* out of jail."

"I knew I liked Apollo for a reason," Frank says unconcernedly.

"In the house," Lydia dictates. "I have some stew on the stove that should warm everyone right back up."

She leads the way inside. Blake, the last one to come in, shivers as the heat mixes with the chill in his bones. I need to be warmed back up myself, which makes me think of Apollo immediately. Since I don't want to disturb him while he's working, I follow my family to the dining room.

The past weekend begins to ride my mind like a backwards cowboy. I wonder just how much I hurt Apollo, and if I can actually do something about it. Ill feelings stick with people, and they usually regurgitate them back at the one that caused them, eventually.

Everyone takes the same seats at the empty table that they occupied earlier except Lydia. She begins dishing out the bowls of stew that she promised, placing them in the center of a saucer with crackers, along with iced tea. My food sits in front of me untouched, my mind with Apollo. My mother takes her seat in father's lap at the head of the table, cupping her hand under his spoon when he tows it to his mouth.

I've never known them to not work together on anything. Apparently, they work together on *everything*, including my love life. My mother claims the only way to tolerate the same person for twenty plus years is to truly become one, or a split is inevitable. She also says to keep those with clumsy fingers, like my father, away from the dishes, and those with the potential to burn the house down, like Blake, away from the kitchen.

"What's on your mind, Lisa Poo?" Blake asks, before spooning the steaming soup in his mouth.

I scratch my head. "Well, I'm wondering how I made Apollo feel when I told him that I could take care of myself. Watching mama and daddy together makes me wonder if I made him feel… used… you know… in the—"

Frank starts to choke on his soup. Lydia taps him in the back gently with an opened palm.

"Say no more, Lisa Poo!" Blake yells. "You're about to kill Pop!"

Blake puts his spoon down in his bowl, and puts his hands up a praying fashion over it. "I promised to tell you about men, didn't I?"

I nod, needing his advice.

"When you told Apollo that you'd rather be independent, you actually said that you only needed him for…" he trails off, looks at my father, and then back at me. "…one thing. Yes, Apollo felt used and he's probably not used to that. Being independent is a good thing, but a real man needs to feel needed. No, he won't mind you working or paying for your own things. When he offers to do it, it's because he wants to feel like he plays a part in your life, mostly as a provider and a protector. Every time you said you could do it, he felt like he had no chance to make you happy, so he left, but I'm sure he knew every move you made."

"I didn't make any until Tuesday."

He frowns. "That was worse. He really felt unnecessary in your world, but he loves you. When you didn't chase him to Utah, he called. When you didn't answer, I'm sure his business came to a grinding halt."

"I thought everything was business as usual after he left."

"Not a chance." He serves himself another mouth full of stew. "He was giving you space to find space for him in your life... and miss him."

"That's what Derek said."

"Where is Derek by the way?" my mother asks then glances around.

Blake snickers. "Probably up Chrys'..."

"Blake Powers!" she warns, shooting him a glance meant to maim.

"Chrys took him to the airport. The rest of the crew is in my den, Lydia," my father supplies the answer, then spoons more stew into his mouth. "So, baby girl's backup has pulled out to chase my sister?"

"Yep," Blake says breezily. "It's just the primary now."

"Derek is not a backup," I say huffily. "He's my friend and I needed one after I pushed Apollo with my independency that apparently, I don't know how to turn off."

My father grins into his empty bowl. "Baby girl, I taught you to be independent until you found the man that earned the right to take care of you. When you did, you rest your weary independent cap. It gets lonely going at it alone all the time, and I don't want you to lose a good man because you're rigid and sticking to the lessons I taught as guidelines to use throughout your life. They're just that... guidelines to have should you need something to fall back on. It's okay to receive, baby girl."

"Now you tell me, daddy," I gripe.

Rumbling laughter erupts from his chest. "Your mother and I never wanted you to meet anyone to take care of you in the first place, Malisa. You are my baby girl and you'll always be that. But since you've obviously met someone that you love and Apollo is proving to be a good man who loves you back, the rest of the lesson is paramount, since he's not leaving here without you. I know I wouldn't."

"You didn't, Frank," Lydia snipes.

He grins up at her. "Damn straight, my love."

She stands up, and starts gathering the empty bowls on the table.

"I got it, mama," I offer, before I stand up, too.

"I got it, Malisa. Go see if Apollo wants something to eat, and take your bowl of stew before it gets cold."

I scoop up the saucer and glass of iced tea, and walk quickly to Apollo's room. I tap on the door with my foot. It opens immediately.

He smiles. "Hey, love."

I get a damn head rush. "I came to see if you wanted something to eat and talk to you a little bit, if you're not busy."

He steps to the side then takes the dishes from my hand. "I'm never too busy for you. Come in, and then I want you show you some things I'm looking at on my laptop."

I walk in, nervous as if I've showed up at his door unannounced, oddly, when this is my parents' home. His nearness is clogging up every sense that I have. The guest bedroom is plain when I consider what Apollo is used to, but I wouldn't change the simple oak furnishings for anything in the world. The queen-sized bed, with short stubby, round posts, thick cream comforter with palm trees and Apollo's laptop, sits in full view of the door. I have to pass through the tiny extensions of wall on each side of the doorway to get an unobstructed view of the room. A flat screen television and its short stand sits behind me, pressed against the wall facing the bed. I can remember every tiny nick, which Blake and I put there, in the tall chest of drawers with lamp positioned on one side of the bed.

Apollo's shaving kit sits on the nightstand on the other side. I sit down on the end of the bed so he can have access to the nightstand, while I watch my reflection in the mirror belonging to the dresser. He shuts the door back with the heel of his shoe. When he sits down beside me and places his food on the nightstand, I turn to him.

"I just had a short talk with my father and Blake, and I need to ask you something."

He sips from his glass, his eyes watching me over the rim. "Okay."

"Did I make you feel used sexually before we split in Vegas?"

Apollo sets his glass down beside his food on the nightstand then gives me his undivided attention. "Yes."

"Well, I'm sorry about that, but you need to get over it because I plan to use your body as much as I can, and my independent streak isn't weakening fast enough. We're still stuck with the good and the bad, which brings me to our next piece of business."

He snorts and shakes his head. "What's that?"

"I need another job. We won't get any work done at your office. Your body will be too close to mine, and I'll want it. Four years is a long time to want someone and I'll be doing my damndest to make up for that, so I still need to quit."

"No," he answers simply.

My shoulders slump. "Apollo—"

"My Lisa, we'll just schedule making love sessions for you, and I'll have a bedroom added to my office with a full bathroom."

"Jesus, Apollo, everyone will know what it's for as soon as the workmen show up. I don't like everyone up in my business, which is why I didn't want to stay here with you *and* my family.

"Everyone will know anyway, when we start to go out on dates from the office, and that's why construction companies don't mind the extra money they make for their discretion and working at night when everyone else has gone home."

"Sweetheart, I appreciate everything you do for me, but I told you that you don't have to go out of your way for me."

"My Lisa, I do. If it's my body that you want in between meetings and working at the office, then it's my body that you'll get. You're not the only one that wishes they could make up for the time we lost while sitting across from each other every day."

"I thought waiting to make love made it greater, *baby*," I mock.

"It does... until it doesn't work."

"Until it doesn't work for *you*, you mean."

"Yes," he says seriously, which just makes us both laugh.

"Well, while I have you in a good mood and we're alone, I have something to confess. You were right about what you said about Blake."

"I know."

"Smartass."

He grins. "I know that, too."

I sober up. "But he isn't going to push his attraction. When we both found him in my bed, I thought he just still need to be validated emotionally."

"He does. Everyone does, but he'd rather be in your life as your brother than risk losing you or your family."

"I'm not even going to ask how you know that, but I know how he feels. I felt the same way about you."

"Until you didn't."

I nod. "Until I didn't. Once you've crossed that line and your heart steps over it with you and gets a taste of what you can have, it's hard to find your way back to where you started. I know my heart wouldn't go, even when I tried to make it."

He reaches for my hand. "I know what Blake would choose to do because I don't have blood family backing me. The choice he made to keep all the Owens in his corner is the one I'd make, too. Or he'd have pursued you way before now. I'm glad your heart won't go back and it won't let you, because *I'm* not going back. I'll do whatever you want to make this work between us, even if that means putting up with Blake… who's spoiled rotten."

"And it's so unfair," I gripe.

"Trust me, love. You've both been spoiled rotten with love. He just appreciates it more because it comes from outside the home that was obligated to provide him with it… and he uses it to his advantage."

"He does that."

"That's what family is for, to take and give more than they should. Speaking of taking, you know Jenna isn't worth the designer tags on her clothes that she buys with her unearned paycheck."

Every muscle in my body locks up. "Apollo, why in hell would you mention your secretary right now, of all times? If you tell me that you've been sleeping with her, I swear!"

"I haven't slept with her ever, baby," he says quickly, but he starts to rub the back of his head, like he does when he's faced with a difficult decision that he doesn't want to face.

There aren't many of those, but firing people is one of them.

I get pissy and stomp my foot. "Oh, come on! You want me to fire her for you, don't you?"

"Yes, please. She's not family or deserves to take when she doesn't give even a tenth back. She'll probably cry and get another three and a half years as my secretary, if I do it."

I guess I know him better than I thought. "You've tried to fire her before, haven't you?"

He glances at me, with a guilty look on his face. "Yes, and you can see how well that worked out."

"You are just full of surprises today," I grumble.

"Look at this way. Life with me will never be boring."

"They weren't good surprises, Apollo. You don't pay me enough for this."

"What's your idea of a raise?"

"I wasn't fishing for a raise. I already got the one I wanted from your PA to your woman, but I will take less responsibility at your company."

"How about I give you the company instead?"

"Jesus, no! That defeats the purpose of not working my ass off every day, and I'd really be running the company singlehandedly because I'd fired damn near every one that works there within the week."

"I have some good people at my company, my Lisa."

"And they're overworked and underpaid because of the ones that slack off all day."

"Okay, so we start to move people out, then up."

"It's not that easy, Apollo. You'd have to work out severance packages and make sure the lower level employees are ready to move up. We'd still be working seven days a week for months trying to put them in place, and I'm just your personal assistant that no one will take seriously."

"They would if you're my vice president."

This is just getting worse.

I sigh.

"No, Apollo. I don't want to live at your company anymore."

"Obviously, you don't know what vice presidents do, do you, my Lisa?"

"I'm sure you're going to tell me."

"They delegate."

"That's what CEO's do, too. I'm the one you delegate to, remember?"

"Damn straight."

"It's true then. The less money you make, the harder you work."

He grins at me, and that's so not a good sign. "Yep, so when can I have your name stenciled on the door of my office with vice president above it?"

"You mean to tell me that I can't even get my own office?"

"No. You're going to be at my side from here on out, where you belong."

"Apollo, you don't think we need some space, to at least miss each other?"

"We'll miss each other, when one of us goes to the bathroom. When we sleep. When you take trips to Colorado that I can't follow on when you take them on the jet, which I'm looking at for you right now."

"A jet!" I start to laugh. "You like giving me reasons to turn you down, don't you?"

He grins arrogantly down on me. "It's when you find something to accept from me that the fun begins."

"I just need your heart, sweetheart… and your body."

He shifts on the bed until his thighs are pressed to mine then drops his arm across my shoulder and along my back, before pulling me into him. "And I need to take care of you, my Lisa. Whatever is mine is yours."

"You're going to make me take it all, aren't you? The vice presidency? The jet? Is there a castle in the works, too?"

"Yep. Thirty miles away from here. I'm looking at potential spots for a land grab, as well. Castles, princes, and princesses need lots of space… or so you told me."

"Speaking of little people with crowns on. We haven't used a condom not one time that we've slept together."

Apollo leans us back until we are laying on the bed then tosses my leg over his. "Do you want me to start using them?"

I snuggle into the crook of his arm. "My clock started ticking when I laid eyes on you. I may be like my mother and can only have one child before my uterus says to hell with that and gives up."

"Even if we have no children, my Lisa, I have the most important person in my world right beside me."

"Then it's official then, no condom."

"Deal, vice president."

I slide up Apollo's body and plant my mouth on his before he thinks of something else in his office to give me, besides his heart.

Epilogue
Eight Months Later

I take a sip of my iced tea, just plain ice cubes and chamomile. If my family or husband-to-be suspected me of drinking anything alcoholic before my wedding, I'd have to run away to avoid the uproar, while eight months pregnant with triplet boys. God knows I haven't been able to run in the last three months. I can barely walk now, and it's almost impossible to get in and out of any mode of transportation lately.

Just getting from my mother's house to my uncle Luke's ranch where the ceremony is going to be held was a major production this morning. I had more hands in my back making sure I didn't fall between the front porch and Apollo's pearl-white Navigator than I have inside me. And God knows my back is wide at this stage of my pregnancy too, but Apollo was parked across the front lawn for the ease of me stepping from the bottom porch step to the running board of the truck.

What was I going to do? Trip over the step up and fall into my seat?

Everyone is still completely overbearing here, I tell you. Apollo has picked up the tendency, as well. Uncle Luke's wife Natalia, a part-time botanist, full-blooded Comanche Indian, and mother to Luke Jr. is no better. As soon as we arrived here, she made me take a seat in my uncle's favorite recliner and forbade me to leave it. I'm sure he didn't appreciate that, if the grimace that appeared on his face at the time is any indication of his feelings. I *am* grateful though. The constant swelling in my feet gets out of control quickly if I stand too long, which makes it feel like I'm walking on balloons.

However, I'd love to be outside on one of the last warm days of autumn, helping my family decorate the gardens that Natalia has been creating for the last two years. She still has another year, and about two acres to landscape and add fountains and wooden benches to, before she can rent the grounds out for events. I'd have waited until then, just to avoid the bloated wedding photos. Apollo nixed that idea when I told him I was two months pregnant. He proposed in Aspen our first night there. He wanted his kids to be born legitimately as Fords, and I do, too.

Yep, he finally got me to ski slopes. I still don't know how to ski like he wanted me to learn, but he's more concerned with getting married in a few hours before I pop. Feels more like a shotgun wedding the more I think about it, even if I fantasized about getting married here one day. As a child, I found infinite things to do here with my imagination, including being a bride. Hopefully, my children will get to play at Blake's and my second favorite childhood place to be, too.

I have another sip of tea, wanting to blow up at least one balloon and attach it to a chair at the reception. Then I can say I had some part in the hard work that's going into my dream wedding. How hard can it be to push down on the level of a helium tank and wait for the latex to blow up? It must be pretty damn difficult because an argument broke out about it this morning. I didn't even get the suggestion of me doing it out of my mouth before Apollo *and* my mother shot me down because I stupidly raised my hand first to get everyone's attention.

Major mistake. I should've just spit the words out. All I've contributed to my wedding is picking out the colors, font for the invitations, the wedding party's attire, and the venue. Now, I'm stuck in the house, watching a theater screen in my uncle's man cave, with my feet up, and being served by whoever ventures in the back door for whatever reason. I make sure to grumble about being unable to participate. Then I go right back to doing nothing… happily. Trust me when I promise that I'll get to blow up that damn balloon though, but I'm not upset about missing my mother ordering everyone around, including the wedding planner and her staff.

Poor people! Better them than me though.

The doorbell for the front door sounds off. It has to be a guest that knows better than to try and find their way alone around the ranch, looking for the gardens that are a half a mile away. They'd probably find the stinky, riding horses first, which is on the other side of the ranch thankfully.

Jesus, how many businesses does one family need, I ask myself, since no one else is around to ask *or* answer the door. I'd be a little irritated with having no one to pull my tank-sized ass out of the chair, if they all weren't working with my mother supervising. They're stressed enough, without me calling them to come eight acres over to help me up, even if they're using a golf cart to get back and forth.

I fight to get out of the chair, with the boys riding my bladder and spine, and consider calling Apollo anyway… or whoever answers their phone first. *You can do this by yourself, Malisa.* After that pitiful pep talk, I get a poke in the ribs before I get to my feet, which takes my breath. I stand up, rearrange the robe that I'm wearing until time to ditch it for my peasant wedding dress. It's made of white satin in a baby doll style for maximum comfort, with thick shoulder straps and round diamonds around the bust, and could pass for a tent.

I waddle around Luke Jr's play pen. I'm only a room away from the front door, but when I reach it, it feels like I've walked a mile. I grab the doorknob to prop on it instead of turning it, while trying to peek through the frosted panes in the door. I get a distorted image of whoever's on the other side, with no idea if it's a man or woman or more than one person.

"Who is it?" I ask before the back door opens in the kitchen.

Oh now, someone shows up. Typical.

"It's Sienna, Malisa," Apollo's mother answers back.

"My Lisa, what are you doing?" he asks worriedly from behind me before his presence swamps the room.

It's bigger than a standard living area, and filled with white contemporary furniture with brown wood trimming. Yet, he manages to fill it up with his essence anyway.

"I'm letting your mother in, babes. What does it look like I'm doing?" I open the door.

He smirks. "You could've called me to do it, sweetheart."

Sienna steps inside, with a garment bag thrown over her arm, and attempts a hug around her grandchildren. I have to bend over before she can get her empty arm around my neck. Hugging my waist isn't an option, and she isn't tall enough to reach over the bulge of my belly to get to me. She's even shorter than me.

Apollo got his height and looks from his father. Sienna is a fragile and pale-looking beauty surrounded by sadness. I sensed it the moment she opened her door to me five months ago, not expecting Apollo to be standing beside me. He was dead serious about giving no warning. I think he was afraid she'd run before he found her, but he won't admit it.

He shouldn't have been worried at all. She's extremely strong and has been living alone since Lazarus' death. They refused to have any more children after Apollo was taken from their life. She recognized him immediately, broke down crying just as fast, and then hauled him into her arms. After he told her she was going to be a grandmother and she'd shown him all his baby pictures that she had framed all over the house, she cried some more.

I thought I wouldn't find a mother more dedicated than Lydia. I'm glad to confess that I am dead wrong. A little bit of Sienna's sadness disappears every time we visit her or she comes to see us wherever we are. She does more coming lately on my jet, since I can't travel and she flat out refused her own from Apollo. I still haven't figured out how to stop him from buying me expensive things, like the seven-carat rock on my finger. It's just as heavy as his children are, and I only drooled over the thing once, after we passed by it in a display window.

Okay, I drooled every time I passed by it in Utah for a month. That still doesn't mean I wanted it.

It doesn't hurt that Sienna's very sweet-natured either, so I'm always glad to see her. Maybe she'll tell me her secret to getting Apollo to accept no at least sometimes.

I grin and sweep her waist-length brunette hair with strands of gray weaving in and out of her bone-straight locks behind her back. "I couldn't leave my future favorite mother-in-law standing on the porch, waiting for someone to get here, Apollo. That is *not* the way to start out the rest of our lives as extended family."

"She's your *only* future mother-in-law, my Lisa, and the only one you're going to get if I have my way," he responds dryly, while waiting for his hug.

Sienna giggles before releasing me to circle her son's waist. She'll never reach his neck. "I wouldn't have minded, Malisa. You really should be resting."

The back door opens, again.

"God, Sienna, you sound like your son," I complain.

She laughs.

"She's right, baby girl," my mother pipes up before crossing the threshold between the kitchen and the living room.

I sigh. "And you sound like Sienna, mama. Three against one. Don't you all feel good about picking on a pregnant woman?"

Uncle Tommy snickers behind Lydia, before stepping around her. "Be fair, Malisa. You have them outnumbered. The load in front of you count as at least six... maybe seven people. That's a big stomach, woman."

"Shut up, Tommy," my father says out of nowhere, before stepping up on the front porch then through the opened door.

"You count as eight by your damn self, Frank," Uncle Tommy responds.

My father shakes his head. "Shut… up… Tommy. Go sit down, baby girl."

"Daddy!" He's supposed to be on my side.

My mother giggles. "Finally, you're of some use with these kids, Frank."

He wraps his arm around her waist and pulls her into his side. "As long as she's pregnant, Lydia, you got my support… but you're on your own again when she gives birth."

She snorts and shakes her head. "Nobody's perfect."

Blake walks through the opened front door. "I got your back, Mama O. Go sit, Lisa Poo. You look unstable… seriously."

"Fine. You all want me to sit? Go bring the helium tank and a balloon."

Apollo groans. "Not this again. Baby, please. That thing is dangerous and can tip over on you." He walks behind me, and has no trouble circling my waist with his long arms.

I lean back into his chest then twist to look up at him. "Helium tank and a balloon are all I'm asking for. You can even hold the tank if you want to."

"I got handcuffs if you need them, Apollo," Blake adds. "We'll attach her to the chair one way or the other."

"Ew, Blake!" Natalia squeals from somewhere in the house, and Luke Jr. mimics her in his adorable toddler tone. "There's no telling who all you've attached those things to!"

"That's not going to work anyway," Uncle Luke says, after appearing out of nowhere. "My chair doesn't have metal rings and I better not find your cuffs attached to nothing and no one in here, Blake. Why are you all standing around anyway? There's work to be done. Malisa, you really need to sit down, honey. I've never seen a belly that big… ever."

"Aw hell," Uncle Tommy starts, "The bear is grumpy. Time to go until he's had his porridge. I'll warn my sisters and Derek when I get back to the gardens to stay away from the house and head the rest of the guests off at the driveway." He turns and leaves the way he came.

The room fills with laughter, just as he intended. I realized for the umpteenth time how much I've missed making these memories with my family. Having Apollo, and soon our own family, to share them with just makes them that much more precious. Now, if I can just get Blake married off.

The End...for now.

Earned by the Billionaire
by Shani Greene-Dowdell

CHAPTER ONE

KAYLA

Good Riddance

The "walk of shame" to my boss's office was always torture. This time, I prayed she wouldn't say anything out the way, as I headed in there to tell her I had to leave early. This particular day wasn't the day for me to tamp back my anger and take the high road. If she got fresh out of her lips, I was going to tell her something not so sweet about her lopsided ass. Well, maybe that's not the nicest thought to have about someone who held my financial future in their hands. But the lady had no redeeming qualities. I wouldn't take it as far as a physical attack, but it most definitely wouldn't fare well for either of us if she tried to humiliate me as she had in the past when I had personal matters come up during office hours.

"I have an emergency at home that I need to deal with immediately," I told Helen when I entered her office after knocking. I just got straight to the point. I didn't have time to hem-and-haw with her. "My job is caught up, and Sandra is covering my phone line," I added, wanting her to know I'd handled my business before I even approached her.

"Kaaaylaaaa," she drew out my name with a sigh. Sitting in her high-back chair, she wore a pair of bifocals and a messy brunette ponytail piled at the top of her head. She peered at me over the rim of her glasses and made a grating sound with her teeth. "What could possibly be going on with you noooowah?"

I tried it.

You see, I attempted to come in here and talk to this lady like a professional, but she was the master at pissing me off.

"What's going on is personal. I prefer not to discuss it with you, Heleeeen." I drew her name out the same way she had done mine, my faux smile never leaving my face. She brought out the petty and childish in me that I thought I'd long since buried. But I did say I wasn't in the mood, didn't I?

"I'm your boss. I have the right to know what's going on before I approve for you to leave."

"Like I said, it's personal. But hold up; let's back up a second. The way you asked 'what could it be *now*' suggests that I've been leaving early often. The only other time I've requested to leave early in the past year was when my mother was sick and needed me to take her to the emergency room."

Helen had been my boss from hell for four years, so I cautiously kept my time off to a minimum. The first time she complained about me having a dental appointment I knew she was a piece of work. And, I knew for a fact that I didn't have a habit of dodging work.

"But you were just out on…" She flipped the calendar hanging on her wall back a few months. "August second with a summer cold."

"That was two months ago, and I had the flu. What do you want me to do when I'm ill? Come in here sick?"

"I suppose it doesn't matter at this point."

Bingo bitch, I guess I can take brain dead off my list of assessments about you. That was what I thought, but I cocked my head to the side and sized her up instead of speaking ugly to her. We had this mean-nice way of speaking to each other, so I hit her with another one of those exchanges.

"Given that we accrue sick time, why did you bring up my sickness from two months ago? Being sick is why the owners give it to us, or am I mistaken?" I held on to the last strand of tact in my being. If this unreasonable banter didn't end in the next few seconds, there was a high chance of me walking out the front door with her ass in my hands. Bosses like Helen made people shoot up the fucking place with no remorse.

"Go ahead and go, Kayla," she said, pushing her glasses back over her nose. "But let me be clear, you can consider yourself warned. The next time that you have to leave midday without a valid excuse will result in a write-up."

"Thank. You. For. Understanding," I said, but not in a nice way. No. I shot the words across the room and straight into her eyes like daggers. Each word for a different eye. If I had cosmic powers that allowed my thoughts to come true, she'd be strung up by the unruly ponytail on her head and hanging from the same nail that held her irrelevant credentials in place on the wall.

"Ugh," I stormed down the hall of Naustram Media Agency, my spiked heels clacking against the shiny, marvel floors every step of the way. "Ju better have a good reason for not going to work today, or else I'm going to lose my fucking mind on him when I get home."

In reality, I'd deflected my anger to Helen. The real culprit, Julius Martin, my live-in boyfriend who I called Ju, had done it again. He'd called in from his temp job and gotten fired again. My best friend and roommate, Pam, called me with the news just minutes ago. She said he was holed up in my bedroom playing video games and, when she asked him about work, he told her that they laid him off. Knowing Ju, that translated into "I didn't get my sorry ass out of bed in time, so they let me go."

I just couldn't believe he was doing this to me after he promised he would do better and made love to me last night to seal that promise. It hurt to know I couldn't trust him to fulfill one simple promise. But this was the last straw. What's love without trust?

I hopped in my car and sped off. On the drive to my apartment, I ran a mental assessment of Ju. I couldn't remember the reason I loved him so much. The thought of him laying out of work, acting like he didn't have a care in the world, irked me like nothing else could. I was too ambitious and put too much hope into him—including defending my love for him to my parents. And what did he do? Hand me a shitload of excuses for him to be lazy, every day.

My relationship with my parents had gone to shambles. They saw straight through him on their first time meeting him. Summed him up in a matter of minutes. Every time I went to Alabama to visit, my father was lecturing me about how I deserved to be treated like a queen. "Baby girl, if a man can't give you this," Dad would say as he pointed at our meal spread out on the table, "then he don't deserve nunna yo' time."

My mother was right along with him, talking about how I didn't make Ju earn me. "Just gave him the whole damn cow for free," she would say as she looked at me with the deepest disappointment in her eyes. Man, I was tired of listening to them hold anti-Ju sermons. They made me feel like choosing to be with Ju was a sad reflection of my character. How could I even combat them, when he refused to give me any ammunition?

I should've waited for a man that was just as ambitious as me to come along. I met Ju at a nightclub and fell for his dimpled smile, smooth brown skin and listening ear. His encouraging kisses and warm embrace cemented my feelings over the following months. But nothing made me fall for him more than his melt in your mouth handsome face and kingly stature—strong jawline, deep set eyes, thick brows and luscious, kissable lips that had the ability to make me forget all of my problems. To me, he was infallible. I overlooked all the negatives and rolled with the punches.

197

But, guess what? He could play that damn video game in the streets from now on. He had to get the hell on. Ju had to be delusional to think he could do this again. I kept telling him that a good work ethic was a requirement for him to be my man. Obviously, he couldn't get with the program. He must've had me completely mixed up with another woman. I mean, what did he think I was running? A free soup kitchen and lodging?

The tires of my 2016 Chrysler 200 screeched as I came to a halting stop in the parking space beside his 1994 Grand Prix. His poor car needed everything to get going daily—water, oil, brake fluid, a jump off. And he was too caught up in video game land to make the eight dollars an hour he needed to buy a battery.

No. He'd rather wait for me to get home so he could use my car, debit card, and gas. I spoiled a grown man for a whole year and created a man-child with me being his woman-mother. Well, no more.

Hell no.

The more I thought about it, the more pissed I got. I couldn't even make the argument that we were actually dating because he couldn't afford to take me anywhere. Quite frankly, he was cool with that. But after today, I wasn't settling for his mediocre love. It just wasn't enough.

"I swear before the throne of God, if Ju is laying on my good sheets playing games, I'm going to act like a damn nut," I mumbled under my breath as I stepped out into the biting Chicago chill.

I rubbed my arms as I entered the warmth of my apartment. Hurrying through the living room, I burst into my bedroom in a fury, and there he lay. All six feet of chocolate fineness splayed across my bed with a game controller resting comfortably in his big, capable hands. Just fine with no purpose. At that very moment, I didn't know what would be worse, coming home and finding him in bed with another woman or finding him laying up there acting like a big kid.

"Bae, what you doing home?" he quickly sat up and asked.

"What am I doing home?" I grasped my temples and rubbed them ferociously. My pulse was so loud I thought the thumping sound was a sure indication that my head was about to pop off. "The fuck are you doing home, Ju? Last time I checked, you had a job that you were supposed to be at today."

Everyone that knew me knew I had a repulsion of spiders and flies. I'd lose my mind if one came near me. Well, Ju was the only human alive that ever made me feel the same way about him. I was unglued as I watched him scramble to get out of bed. I just expected so much more from him, and he gave so little.

"Bae, calm down and let me explain," he said as he muted Dragon Quest with the hand controller, extinguishing the annoying noise that was blasting through the console.

I stood by the door huffing in anguish, my shoulders rising and falling as I tried to keep myself from rearranging his stupid face. Ju got up and walked over to me. He attempted to upturn my face so that I was looking into his eyes, but I yanked my face out of his palm.

"I'm not calming down. I had to put up with my boss' shit just to come home and check on your grown ass. To see if it was true that you actually decided not to go to work today. And, low and behold, you're laying up in here chilling like I work for the both of us. How do you plan to build anything with me when you don't even show up? Do you think I'm supposed to support you?"

"No, I don't think that." He grabbed my hands and pulled me to him. "I just want a better jo—"

"Don't!" I used strength I didn't know I had to push him away. I glared at him while pointing my finger to let him know not to approach me again. "Don't run me that bullshit about what you want. You've had at least ten job assignments in the past few months, and you haven't made good on one of them. So to say that you want something better is just a lie. Ain't nobody looking for you while you're laying in your pajamas playing games all day. To get

199

something, you're going to have to get up off your ass, get out of this apartment, and get it. Period."

"Kayla, will you just listen? Damn. All this attitude you're giving me is just unnecessary. You're just pissing me off."

"Oh, you're pissed?"

"Yeah, I'm pissed because you act like I'm not trying."

"You aren't. Now, I want you to act like you understand what I'm about to say. Tune in carefully because I'm about to piss you off even more. Since your actions have spoken for you, check out mine."

I walked over to the closet and pulled down all of his Polo shirts that were lined up neatly. Who's lucky enough to have starch pressed expensive shirts lined up, in every color, when they don't even have a job? Ju, that's who.

I tossed each shirt down onto the floor, followed by his jeans that I just had dry cleaned.

"Kayla, don't do that. You're messing up my dry cleaning."

"I'm done with this shit. I want you and your stupid shirts out of here, now!"

He stormed over to me and used his strength to encircle me into his arms, the same arms that held me in place as he bewitched my body the night before. With a bear hug grip around me, he said, "You don't mean that, Kayla. I want to give you the world, and I have been trying. You just don't give me credit for what I do around here."

"Oh, honey, I mean every word I'm saying to you…" I pushed away with all the strength within me, causing him to loosen his grip on me. "And I do mean every word. You and me, we are done. I don't want you doing anything around here anymore. All I want is for you to get out of here!"

It was just like Ju to clutch on to the very little handiwork and housekeeping that he did in this apartment. He would never get the point that he needed to go somewhere and clock in to work.

"I thought you loved me," he said, looking confused.

"I did."

"Oh, you did, but you don't now?" he asked.

"No, because suddenly the definition of love is sinking in, and this is not it," I said, pointing from me to him.

"Why're you acting like this?"

"Just leave, please!" This was my first time telling him to leave. I'd been pleading with him to do the right thing. But as I pointed to his clothes in the closet, letting him know that he needed to get to packing, he finally understood his fate.

"Where am I gonna go? My family isn't gonna let me move in, and you know that. You're all I got, Kayla."

"You should've acted like I was all you had and fought for me like you wanted to keep me. Since you didn't do that, where you go is not my problem," I said, trekking to the kitchen to grab a big trash bag for his belongings.

I hate that it came to this. But I refused to shoulder the burden for a whole human that I didn't give birth to, not anymore. Julius wasn't my child. It was high time that we both figured that out.

"Go talk to your mother about moving in with her. I'm not her though," I said when I walked back into the bedroom with the box of trash bags.

He was sitting on the bed holding his head. He reluctantly took the trash bags out of my hand and walked over to the closet and started stuffing his clothes in the bag. Ever so often, his light brown eyes collided with mine, looking pitiful.

A tiny morsel of regret traveled through me, only to be stamped out by the sound of the video game unpausing itself. The irritating music caused my stomach to churn in disgust. I did have a lot of love for Ju, but he wasn't the man for me. I'd held on, hoping that he would prove me and my parents wrong. That never happened.

Hell, I wanted kids of my own someday. What would it look like for him to be sitting on the sofa playing the games the kids should be playing, while I worked to provide for our family? What would that teach my sons, my daughters? Putting Ju out was the right decision, and I'd be happy when he left.

An hour later, he walked to the door carrying his last bag over his shoulder. "I'm sorry Kayla. I should've gone harder for you. I miss you already," he said, pleading with his eyes for me to give him a second chance.

"I'm going to miss you too, Ju. We just aren't on the same page and the same line right now. I hope you get it together and do better for yourself," I said from the heart.

"I will. You'll see," he promised, then put his bag down. His eyes pleaded for a parting hug, a conversation or something.

I opened my arms and offered him a hug, deciding to put my animosity aside for the moment. Inhaling the sweet residue of his fresh mint body wash, it felt right to rest against his firm muscles while being encompassed by his warmth. But this would be my last time, and my mind reconciled that fact.

"Bye." I strolled over to the door and held it open for him to walk out.

He got to the top step and looked back at me.

"Can you give me a jump?" he asked, looking ashamed to have to ask.

"Yeah."

This is exactly what I'm talking about, I thought as I walked back into my apartment to grab my keys. Ju having to ask for a jump off was all the more reason this pitiful excuse of a relationship was over. What kind of man lays down when he has so many reasons to get up? If not for me, he should have done it for himself.

Good riddance.

Read More on Amazon.com

www.ingramcontent.com/pod-product-compliance
Lightning Source LLC
Chambersburg PA
CBHW051508170626
46811CB00002B/700